REBECCA BISCHOFF

Hole in the Rock

Immortal Works LLC
1505 Glenrose Drive
Salt Lake City, Utah 84104
Tel: (385) 202-0116

Cover Art by bookcoverzone.com

This book is a work of fiction. Names, characters, businesses, organizations, places, events and incidents either are the product of the author's imagination or are used fictitiously. Any resemblance to actual persons, living or dead, events, or locales is entirely coincidental.

ISBN 978-1-953491-12-1 (Paperback)
ASIN B08T81J77Z (Kindle Edition)

For my Dad, Jack Israel. Thanks for all the weekend trips to unusual and out-of-the-way places!

The dead deer on the billboard stared at me. Okay, he was only a photo printed on a giant vinyl banner. But he still got to me.

When I reached down to take the can of spray paint out of my pocket, my ladder wobbled and I screamed and swung my arms like I was dancing.

"Are you okay, Lizza?" Brooklyn called up to me.

Bracing my hands against the billboard, I risked looking down while my heart tap-danced in my chest. My best friend squinted up at me from under her thick yellow bangs.

"I'm okay as long as you hold on better than that," I said. "I thought I was road kill for a second."

"Sorry," Brooklyn said. "Are you sure you want to do this?"

"I'm sure," I said. "I'm just going to change the number."

A VW bug zipped past us and honked, and I jumped. It was only 6:00 a.m., but tons of people were already rushing by on the highway. Since the sun was almost up, I'd have lots of witnesses if I didn't get a move on. Even this early in the morning the air was warm, but the heat wouldn't stop a single person from going outside. In Moab, Utah you did outdoor stuff like hiking, mountain biking, swimming, rock climbing, and river rafting—no matter how hot it got. Or climbing up ladders to make a few changes to a billboard. Stuff like that.

"Just hold the ladder steady, okay?" I turned back to the poor, dead deer. He'd never asked to get killed and have his head stuck onto someone's wall. And *I'd* never asked to have a dad who was a taxidermist—a guy who stuffed and stitched together dead animals, making them into really gross decorations. I hated Dad's job with every bone in my body and every hair on my head.

Frowning, I grabbed the tiny can of white paint I'd jammed into my back pocket. It only took a couple of quick sprays to do what I needed to do.

"Look out below!" I yelled, and dropped the can.

"Ouch!" Brooklyn shouted. Then she laughed. "Just kidding."

Blowing on the paint to make sure it was dry enough, I pulled a Sharpie marker from my other back pocket. Carefully, I drew new numbers on the billboard to replace the ones I'd just painted over. Now, anybody who tried to use the phone number on the sign to call my dad would get somebody else.

"Hey, that looks pretty good, Lizza," Brooklyn said. "You can hardly tell it was painted over. Is that a real phone number?"

"Yep. It's for Lila's Dial-A-Fortune," I said. Brooklyn burst out laughing. Lila LaRue was an old lady in town who read cards to tell the future. She'd probably be thankful for more phone calls. Not that I'd ever tell her it was because of me.

Done, I patted the deer's nose. I hoped nobody would notice the changed numbers for a really long time.

I tightened my grip on the ladder and stepped down one rung.

A dog barked from somewhere close to us and Brooklyn shrieked in surprise and let go. The ladder swayed like I was in an earthquake. I screamed, wind-milling my arms.

"Hold on!" Brooklyn shouted.

Scrabbling to grab onto something, *anything*, I caught the sign in front of me, my fingernails tearing into its vinyl surface. After a couple of very long seconds, I got my balance back. I scrambled down the ladder and reached the safety of the ground, breathing hard. And then I looked up.

"Oh, no," I moaned.

My nails had pulled away part of the deer's face and torn off one of the letters. My dad's billboard now had a one-eyed deer on it. And below that, it read:

Crap Taxidermy

Trophies for a reasonable price. Call (435) 555-7462

"Oh, *fudge cakes!*" My last name is pronounced "Cray-po," but, well, it's a name that's spelled like the word "crap," with an "o" stuck on the end. Of course, that last letter just had to be the one I'd torn off.

"The whole sign is ruined," Brooklyn whispered, putting an arm around me.

"I know," I said with a groan, brushing my dark hair out of my eyes.

I bit my lip. My mom was always telling me to *manage*. Manage my temper. Manage my grades a little better. Manage the things in my life I didn't like by doing something to change them. Well, that was all I was trying to do today. I wanted to change the world and make it safer for animals, but I ended up with a massive *fail*.

We carried the ladder away from the sign and hid it

behind a clump of cottonwoods. When we were done stashing it out of sight, we headed for our bikes. Brooklyn kept looking over her shoulder like she expected someone to catch us any second.

"When are we going to get the ladder back to Tona? It's way too light out, now," she said.

Tona was my neighbor and friend, and we borrowed his tools all the time. Usually, we asked first, though.

"I'll come back to get it when it gets dark. Then I'll put it inside his garage," I said.

"All by yourself?" Brooklyn put her hands on her hips. "We barely made it here with the two of us balancing that thing between both of our bikes. If anyone saw us, they probably thought a circus was in town."

I giggled. "And we were a couple of acrobats."

"Or a couple of clowns," my friend said with a smirk.

"Well, I figured I'd walk back when it gets dark and drag the ladder behind me."

I shrugged. "It will take me forever, but using the bikes to carry it was too hard. And I think it'll be a lot less noticeable this way."

"Good." Brooklyn grabbed her water bottle and took a long drink.

Squinting through the leafy branches overhead, I took one last look at the ruined sign. "Crap Taxidermy," I said out loud.

Brooklyn started to laugh, but since she'd just taken a drink, she spit-sprayed water onto my shirt. And then we both laughed so hard tears ran down our faces.

"It *is* funny," Brooklyn said, gasping for air. "But sorry about your shirt."

"Oh, I'll get you back some time," I promised her.

Her green eyes crinkled at the corners and her summer

tan flushed deeper as she smiled. "Bring it on," she said, giggling.

We finally got going, bumping along the stony ground as we headed home. I kept looking at Brooklyn's new Diamondback mountain bike. It was such a sweet ride. My thrift store Huffy was a real piece of junk next to her bike.

"Your dad's going to see the sign sooner or later," Brooklyn said, when we finally made it to a paved road. "Do you think he'll ever figure out who did it?"

We reached Brooklyn's street and skidded to a stop. "He won't know it was us," I said. "He'll just blame teenagers. Or tourists." At least, I hoped he would.

My friend gave me a tiny smile. "I guess."

"But thanks for helping me, Brooks," I said. "I mean it. I couldn't have done it without you."

"That's what best friends do, right?" Brooklyn leaned from her bike to give me a hug.

I hugged her back, turned and stood on the bike pedals, and pumped toward my street. I yelled, "Toenails!"

Brooklyn didn't answer. I blinked and slowed down. Ever since we'd met, we did this thing called "words of randomness." If one of us said a random word, the other had five seconds to pull a different word or two out of her brain. My bestie was so good at our word game she never needed all five seconds. Her answers always came in a flash. But now Brooklyn was quiet. Uh oh. Maybe she was more worried than I thought. Could she be mad at me for dragging her into this?

My stomach fluttered as I rode away, but by the time I got halfway down the block, Brooklyn yelled, "Fluffy unicorn feet!"

I grinned. My friend couldn't possibly be mad if she did the random word thing with me.

Humming to myself, I sped up and turned onto my street. In less than a minute I was pedaling up our driveway. I chained my bike to the porch and chewed on a fingernail. I never meant to tear up my dad's sign. I only wanted to change the number on it.

Plopping down on the porch steps, I fanned my hot face. My father just didn't understand. He loved to hunt and often came home with some dead animal in his truck. Mom was okay with it, but not me. I didn't even eat meat. Not since I was five and my Grandma Thora killed a chicken in front of me and then expected me to eat cut-up pieces of it. After she fried it, of course.

Glancing down, my t-shirt made me cringe. It had the M&M logo on it. Mom got it for me just last week, saying it reminded her of when I was little. Her nickname for me then used to be M&M. Mischief Maker.

Well, I'd just made a whole lot of mischief. I only hoped nobody would find out.

After last night's rainstorm, the warm air smelled of sagebrush. Sunrise made the world turn gold and the storm had washed the dust from everything, so all the old houses around me sparkled. Down the street, our neighbor Mr. Stricker was already out mowing his square patch of lawn. The elderly man saw me. I gulped. He waved with a gnarled hand. I waved back and ducked my head, hoping he'd forget seeing me come home on my bike, having obviously been somewhere else so early in the morning.

Mr. Stricker's thick glasses glinted in the sunlight as he kept glancing in my direction. Of course he wouldn't forget about seeing me. The Strickers were the busybodies of our street. The curtains of their front window twitched the second anyone stepped outside.

Taking a deep breath, I forced myself to look away from the nosy neighbor and made up a haiku in my head. I'd been doing that ever since Mom taught me about the short poems. She kept telling me the verses were supposed to be about nature, but I wrote haikus about everything. Why not? It helped me think.

I made sure that each line had the exact number of syllables they were supposed to have: five for the first line, seven for the second, and five again for the third line.

I climbed to the sign,
but almost fell, and it tore.
What will my dad say?

Light footsteps padded up from behind. I smiled as my little brother, wearing faded red shorts, put his arms around me and squeezed. His name was Theodore, but we called him Dore. Dore's hugs were the best. Even though he was almost six, he didn't talk much. It didn't matter to me, though. He still had lots of ways to tell us he loved us. I pulled him onto my lap and he snuggled his dark, curly hair on my shoulder.

When the sun inched higher it got too hot, so we went inside where Mom was watching TV.

Act casual, I told myself.

"Hi, Mom." I plopped next to her on our sofa that used to be lime green but was now the color of boogers. I picked at some stuffing that spilled from a hole in the armrest. Dore ran to the kitchen.

"Where's Dad?" I asked.

"He had to go somewhere," Mom said.

"Oh. When will..." I froze. A huge spider, one with long, fuzzy legs and a body almost the size of my hand, crept along the armrest of the couch. One of its legs gently tapped on Mom's arm. She looked down. She flew from the couch, screaming, and jumped up on a chair.

"Lizza," she wailed.

I gently scooped the tarantula into my hands and stroked the orange and red markings on her back.

"Rosie would never hurt you," I said. "I'm sorry, I must have forgotten to put the lid on her cage again."

"Out!" Mom yelled. "She goes outside!"

"But Mom—"

"Go!" Mom pointed to the door. "She stays in the shop or I'm smashing her with the biggest pan I can find in the kitchen."

"I'll get her cage," I said with a sigh. Once Rosie was back inside her little house, a glass box with a plastic lid, I picked it up. Rosie waved her legs at me, like she was telling me she understood. I'd found her a few weeks ago on a hike in the desert outside of town. Dad was okay with her but Mom wasn't. At least she'd let me keep Rosie in my room. Until today.

"Sorry, sweetie," I said. "You have to live with the dead animals. Mom said."

I went outside and headed to the small square building that served as our garage. Well, it used to be our garage until two months ago when my dad started his taxidermy business. My stomach got the fluttery, sick feeling it did every time I had to go in there.

"Well, here we are." I pushed the door open. The eyeball wall glared at us. Brown and yellow glass eyes, from tiny ones to eyes the size of jawbreakers, hung in neat rows up and down an entire wall. Dad stuck them up there so he could choose the ones he needed without having to go through a box. File cabinets stood in a row along another wall, full of the creepy metal tools Dad needed for his new job. A big freeze-dry machine, looking kind of like a giant washing machine with a glass window, stood in the corner. Deer, elk, and bison heads hung on walls and laid on work tables—along with a couple of dead fish tacked to boards, and somebody's deceased poodle.

I shuddered.

"Try not to look at them," I told Rosie, clearing a place

for her on Dad's longest table. "I'll let you run around on the grass later," I promised my fuzzy friend. I bolted for the shop door while shivers ran up and down my back. That place gave me the creeps!

Outside, I sat on our porch swing, kicking my legs. The gentle rocking movement helped my heart slow down. I just didn't get my dad, and he sure didn't get me. Dad actually thought I'd *like* his new job!

You love animals, he'd said. *This is your kind of thing.*

Leaning back, I stared up at the spider webs in the corner of the porch. I did love animals, but I loved the ones that were *alive,* not dead and stuffed. My kind of thing would be to open an animal shelter, not make weird wall art out of dead pets.

I kicked my legs harder and made the porch swing bump against the house. Ever since I could remember, trying out new jobs was what my dad *did.* He'd been a cook, a security guard, and a financial advisor. He'd even considered getting his pilot's license. But then, he decided he had to become a taxidermist. *Barf!*

That's why I changed the numbers on Dad's sign. If Dad's business slowed down, even a little, maybe he'd decide it wasn't working. And if it wasn't working, maybe he'd do something else. But I just had to get clumsy and ruin the whole dumb billboard.

Crumb buns! Waiting for Dad to find out about the sign was going to be the worst.

Mom called me in for breakfast, but before I got up, Noah, one of our neighbor's kids, ran over to me. The tow-headed kid was three and always "finding" invisible animals for me.

"I got a bird." He held out his empty hand. He looked

up at me with huge eyes the color of the desert sky and waited.

"Ooh, it's so pretty," I said. "What kind of bird is it?"

The kid looked down at his palm. "A red bird. Here." He pretended to put the bird in my hand and I pretended to stroke its feathers. "I'll take good care of it," I promised him.

"Okay, bye!" He leapt down the steps and ran back to his house. I waved before heading inside for some food.

Mom poured cereal for me and handed me the almond milk. Dore drank a nutrition shake—my parents gave up a long time ago trying to get him to eat regular food. While we ate, Mom reminded me that I couldn't rescue any more animals the whole summer. She came up with that rule after I brought Rosie home.

"I'm okay with the birds with broken wings and the stray cats and dogs, but *that* thing? Ugh. After summer's over, if you do find any more animals, they can only have four legs," she said. "Or two."

"That's not fair." I flicked a piece of cereal with my finger. It pinged against the wall and Mom made me go pick it up. "Dad can bring home all the animals he wants."

Mom laughed. "But they stay in the shop, and they don't pee all over the house."

"Yeah, because they're dead."

Sighing, Mom ruffled my hair. "Just don't forget—no more rescuing this summer. It was hard enough to find a permanent home for that last mutt."

"I know." I ducked my head. Gary, a bulldog with one missing leg, was a sweetheart, but no matter what we tried he was impossible to house train. Dad finally took him to the Humane Society. I'd only agreed because the place kept the animals forever, they didn't put them to sleep. I hated to lose Gary. He used to sit with his droolie head on my leg while I did my homework, but I did get tired of mopping up after him.

"At least tarantulas don't pee on your floor," I said, carrying my bowl to the sink.

Mom made me do the dishes for being a smart aleck.

Mom went into the living room and checked under the couch cushions for more tarantulas before she'd sit down. Then she, Dore, and I watched TV for a while. After a couple of minutes, my brother jumped up and ditched his shorts. Mom chuckled but I cringed. I loved my cute brother, but he really needed to learn to keep his clothes on. And, I totally wished he would talk already. People asked us lots of questions about it.

After Mom wrestled Dore's shorts back on, she wrapped him in his favorite afghan, an old orange blanket with a bunch of holes in it. Grandma Thora—chicken killer Grandma Thora—had crocheted it when she was young, like when T-Rex's were alive, or something.

"So, where did Dad go so early?" I folded my legs under me to keep them from bouncing. "Um, is something wrong?" I held my breath.

"*Wala,*" Mom said. "Nothing, honey."

Whew. My shoulders sank in relief.

"I know what *wala* means," I said, chuckling. My mom always translated anything she said in Tagalog to English. It helped her non-Filipino friends, but *I* didn't need her to do it. After all, I'd heard Mom speak her native language all my life. I wasn't too bad at speaking it myself. I practiced every week by having video chats with Mom's mother, my *lola*, or grandma, Marita.

Mom yawned and ran a hand through her smooth, dark hair. I patted the tangled nest straggling down my back and sighed.

"Why can't I have your hair, Mom?" I asked like I had a gazillion times before.

My mother tilted her head as she studied me. Her dark eyes turned up at the corners, making her look happy, even though too many sleepless nights staying up with my insomniac little brother left her with dark circles that never quite seemed to go away. The tired eyes never made her any less beautiful, though. Her golden-brown skin was smooth, and her hair always did what she wanted it to. Mine tangled in knots and flew around my face just to annoy me, no matter what I did to it.

"You would if you'd comb it once in a while." Her eyes sparkled.

"I *do* comb my hair," I said. "Well, most of the time."
Mom laughed.

"I just wish I looked more like you." My lighter skin came from my dad, who had blond hair and a face as round and pale as the full moon. He was a lot taller than Mom, and it looked like I was going to be that way, too, and soon. My legs never seemed to stop growing.

"You look like *you*, Lizza," Mom said, "and I wouldn't want it any other way."

Smiling, I fished the remote from under the couch and changed the TV to a country music channel. A Clint Brown music video played. I picked off my blue glitter nail polish while we listened to twanging guitars. Dad talked about this guy, his favorite music star, almost like they were best buds. He'd say things like: *Clint just bought himself a new ranch,* or *His last song only got to number two. People don't know good music anymore.*

Mom swiped the remote and changed to a local cable channel, and Dad's new commercial came on. I'd never seen it before. My eyes widened. Even while recording a commercial that lots of people were going to see, he wore his favorite faded jeans and a t-shirt that read, "Meat is a vegetable." The wobbly way the camera moved made me dizzy while I watched my dad show off his taxidermy shop and his latest trophies.

I threw a couch pillow at the screen.

"Ew! That is mor-ti-fy-ing." I said, dividing up each syllable of the word just in case Mom didn't get how embarrassed I was. "And it's so gross! Why did Dad have to become a taxidermist? There's nothing wrong with being a bus driver. Or a cook."

Mom laughed and made me pick up the pillow. "He's wanted to do this for a long time, honey."

I sat down with a huff, hugging the faded pillow to my chest.

Mom stroked my hair.

"Remember, not everyone thinks the same way you do," she said softly. "Like lots of your friends. And your family. But you still love them, don't you?"

"I guess."

Mom laughed and finger-combed a couple of tangles out of my hair.

"Ouch!" I said.

We watched TV for an hour while the sun rose higher in the turquoise sky and the world woke up around us. Dore fell asleep in Mom's lap. She played with his hair and gazed at the screen with sleepy eyes. I was breathing easy when the screen door banged open and my dad ran in.

I sat up straight while my heart jumped around inside me like a barefoot kid trying to cross hot pavement in July.

Dad wore the biggest grin ever, so he must not have seen his sign. I leaned back so I'd look relaxed. I even threw in a fake yawn.

"Great news," Dad said, his blue eyes shining. "Roger agreed to the deal, and we got his lawyer out of bed so we could sign the papers. Let's go out to breakfast to celebrate!"

"We already..." Mom stopped after looking at Dad's face. "Sure," she said. "Let's celebrate." She got up and hugged Dad. "I didn't think he'd sign."

"Well, Roger didn't want to give up the place, but he's never around, and Grandpa always insisted it stay in the family, so it's ours! Your parents, Lizza, are now the official owners of Hole N' the Rock!"

"What?" I blurted. "We *own* Hole N' the Rock? But Uncle Roger—"

"Agreed to sell at a price we could afford," Dad said. "It was a loss for him, but Aunt Ruby chewed him out until he agreed. He lives in Oregon, for Pete's sake! He only comes maybe once a year and expects his employees to run everything without his help. It's been losing money for ages. We're going to turn the place around."

I stared, speechless. I also prayed for a meteorite to smash into my house.

Hole N' the Rock wasn't a hole. It was a cave south of town, dug into a huge red sandstone formation almost as big as the state of Rhode Island. That cave used to be where my dad's grandfather, Albert, lived with his wife, Gladys. My great-grandparents. They'd made themselves a home by blasting the place with dynamite until they got a hole big enough to live in. The house-hole was painted and carpeted inside and even had running water and electricity. And a bunch of dead, stuffed animals. Great-Grandpa Albert had been a taxidermist.

I'd never told anyone my dad's grandparents were the ones responsible for that place. Not even Brooklyn. It was just too embarrassing. Almost as embarrassing as the souvenir shop next to the cave-house that sold plastic jewelry, polished geodes, and postcards. With our Uncle Roger hardly ever there, it was easy to pretend my family didn't have a connection to that tourist trap.

I bit my lip. Seventy-five years ago, my great-grandfather painted giant white letters right onto the red stone, spelling out the awful name he gave the place. He even painted a huge arrow that pointed down to the turnoff from the road. Ha. Like anyone could miss a rock formation almost as tall as a five-story building! What always confused me was why Great-Grandpa Albert spelled the word "in" as a giant "N," with an apostrophe *after* it.

I covered my face and groaned. My family now owned the tackiest tourist trap in the state of Utah—no, in the entire United States of America. Maybe even the world.

And I'd thought the dead animals were bad.

I decided a long time ago that heaven would smell like the Moab Diner. When we got to our favorite booth, I took in a good whiff of fried food and managed a tiny smile. I never ate dead pig, of course, but I still loved the smoky smell of bacon. So sue me.

"Hey, guys," the waiter called as we squeezed into our favorite booth. "Be there in a second."

I sank a little lower in my seat. Our neighbor, Tona—the owner of the borrowed ladder—happened to be a waiter at the diner as a side job. When he wasn't at work there, he wrote for the local paper. He was also a good friend, who lived just two houses away from us.

I plopped my elbows on the sticky table and reminded myself to return the guy's ladder before he got home from work.

"Wanna hear the specials or have the usual?" our neighbor asked while he handed around glasses of ice water. He had to bend down to reach the table. Tona managed to tower over Dad, something not many other people we knew could do.

"What's up, Lizza? You okay?"

I usually liked chatting with Tona. Even though I was barely twelve, he didn't talk down to me like some adults did. But I was still in shock after Dad's Big News. I couldn't think of what to say, so I shrugged.

Dad filled him in and I held my breath, waiting for Tona's reaction.

He blinked a couple of times and his lean, brown-skinned face showed surprise. "Wow," he said, once my Dad took a breath. "You guys are related to the old guy who made that cave-house?"

"Oh yeah," Mom said, trying to keep Dore from once again taking all his clothes off in public. He giggled while she shoved his Iron Man t-shirt back over his head. "That's us."

"Well, uh, congratulations," Tona finally said, glancing at me. His dark eyes were open wide. He got it, even if Dad didn't.

Sorry. Tona mouthed the word at me. I tried to smile at him, but all I could manage was a weird grimace that probably made me look like I was about to cry.

Tona brought us our usual. Dad got a piece of cow served with fries and baby chickens—eggs. Mom ordered fruit cups for herself and me.

"Want to try a bite?" Dad asked me, holding out a piece of bloody steak stuck on the end of his fork. Every day, he tried to get me to eat meat. Every. Single. Day.

I frowned and pulled away, shaking my head.

Then Tona brought Dore his usual meal, even though we hadn't ordered one.

"I figured you guys just forgot," he said when Mom raised her eyebrows.

"Let's see if he'll eat it," Mom said. Dore's usual was a sliced banana, Cheetos, and ketchup. Tona always set the food up the way my brother liked it, with the Cheetos left in the open bag, the banana slices in neat piles, and the blob of ketchup in the exact middle of the plate.

After eyeing the plate for a minute, Dore smiled, dipped a banana slice in his ketchup, and ate it.

"Yes," Tona said with a big smile. "I know my guy." He held out his hand to Dore and they did a fist bump.

It was sweet, but I couldn't stop thinking about Dad's announcement. Everyone was going to know my family owned Hole N' the Rock. My insides chilled like I'd just jumped into a frozen lake. Would I have to *work* there? Sell Betty Boop postcards and cowboy-boot night lights to tourists from Germany?

"You can work there, Lizza," Dad said, like he was a psychic reading my brain waves. "I wanted a business the whole family could do together. This is perfect." He wiped his mouth with the back of his hand and took another bite. He kept talking while he chewed. "You can help lead the tours inside the house. I bet your friends will be jealous!"

The tours. I groaned. Guided tours were led every hour from nine to five to show off the Cave-house of Wonders.

"Kill me now," I mumbled under my breath. I put my head down on the table. Maybe Brooklyn's parents would consider adopting me. Wait... I sat up.

"Does this mean you won't be doing your taxidermy stuff anymore, Dad?" I asked.

If running Hole N' the Rock meant my dad planned to give up stuffing dead animals, then maybe things wouldn't be so bad. I could still pretend my family had nothing to do with the place. Besides, my parents couldn't force me to work there. Or could they?

"Nope," Dad said with a big grin. He ate another forkful of steak. "I'm not giving up on my taxidermy business. I mean, it's a family tradition and all. Grandpa Albert would be proud."

"Oh." My mini spark of hope fizzled out. I leaned my

chin on my hand. Dore grabbed my leg, which was another way he gave hugs.

"Hello," a woman said, interrupting the misery of my new and embarrassing life. I glanced up at a face I recognized. It was Mrs. Barlow. The chubby, brunette woman who always wore huge round glasses was Dore's kindergarten teacher from last year.

Mom straightened her shoulders and her face stiffened. She'd never really liked Mrs. Barlow, who kept asking my parents to let the school to do a bunch of testing on my brother. Like I'd already said, Dore still didn't talk, and he was almost six. But he was smart. We knew that, but I guess not everyone else did.

Mrs. Barlow and my parents chatted a little. Dad, of course, told her his news and Mrs. Barlow grinned like it was the best thing ever that my family now owned a tourist trap.

When Dad finally stopped to take a breath, Mom cut in and said we were late for something. Mrs. Barlow said goodbye and walked back to her table.

"She's only trying to help, Daphne," Dad whispered once the woman was out of earshot. "Don't let her get to you, honey."

"She wants to give our son tests so she can put labels on him." Mom's eyes filled with tears and she sniffed and blinked them away. "Let's not talk about this here, okay?"

So, we didn't. Dad wolfed down the rest of his cow, which by now was cold, and Mom cuddled Dore. Once, I caught Tona's eye and he winked at me. On any other day, it would have made me smile. And maybe blush. Just a little. Tona was cute.

I stuck one elbow onto the table and propped my head on one hand. I speared a bit of watermelon on my fork, but my stomach churned at the idea of eating. With a sigh, I dropped my fork back into the fruit cup. A watery glob of melon splattered onto Dad's shirt.

Dore laughed. He grabbed a fistful of grapes from Mom's plate and threw them at Dad. He was always up for a good food fight.

"No, Dore," Mom said, trying to catch my brother's hands, but the kid was too fast for her. Mrs. Barlow was walking by our booth when a greasy handful of fried potatoes flew into the air and hit her chest. A blob of ketchup dribbled down her shirt.

"It's all right," she said, taking the wad of napkins Dad handed her and waving away his apologies. "This isn't the worst thing I've ever been hit with." She turned to Mom and smiled. "Can I call you later, Mrs. Crapo? We need to talk about this sweet kid, here. He needs specialized therapy, and we can get that for him."

"No, thanks." Mom shoved her chair away from the table. "Let's go, guys."

Dad tossed some bills on the table and we left. We rode in silence for a minute. Mom pulled up a cartoon on her phone and handed it to Dore. Her lips were clamped tight. We all knew better than to try to talk to her when she was in such a bad mood.

Without warning, Mom giggled and after a second, Dad joined in. His laughter grew until it was almost a roar, and his face glowed as red as a Norwegian tourist who'd fallen asleep in the sun.

I couldn't join in the fun. What was there to laugh at? And where were we going? I figured it out the minute we turned onto the highway. Dad was taking us to visit the new family business.

Cheese and crackers, I cursed to myself.

"Great shot, Dore," Mom finally said. "I don't hate Mrs. Barlow, but I did have to laugh when ketchup dripped down her shirt." Dad wiped his streaming eyes. Dore smiled, but his eyes never left the cartoon picture of Krazy Kat on the tiny screen in his hands.

"Let's go look at our new business, okay?" Mom said. "I hear we have quite a lot of work to do."

"We do," Dad said. "You sure you're up for it, Daph?"

Mom took Dad's hand. "You bet I am. *Mahal kita.*"

"*Mahal kita,*" Dad answered. *I love you* in Tagalog.

"Can I borrow your phone, Mom?" I asked.

"If Dore will let you turn off his cartoon," she said. Dore did, after I gave him a bag of stale Cheetos I found under the seat.

"Tell all your friends," Dad told me when I started to tap on the screen of the phone. He caught my eye in the rearview mirror and winked at me.

I ducked my head and texted as fast as I could. Of course, I told Brooklyn what was going on, but I didn't tell her I was directly related to the people who'd built the place. I just couldn't. But I told her my dad bought Hole N' the Rock.

For real??? She answered.

Yes, I texted. *Can I move in with you? Please? It's so humiliating!*

Brooklyn's answer was not what I wanted to hear. *I like that place. Could B fun! I have my piano lesson now. Call U l8TR. Lemon drops!*

Crusty crumbs, I typed. And then I ate one of Dore's stale Cheetos. I ducked down super low in my seat so nobody would see me when we got to the most mortifying place on the planet, while I composed another haiku.

House of rock and dust,
A shop selling plastic junk.
What was Dad thinking?

Well, no matter what Dad thinks, I will not *work there, I* promised myself.
Ever!

I waited by myself outside the souvenir shop. My parents and Dore were taking the "official" cave-house tour, but I refused to join them.

Yawning with boredom and fanning my sweating face, I wandered through the sculptures scattered around outside. My great-grandfather had made some of them out of junk. After he died, some local guy had made even more. These sculptures stood inside the cactus gardens at Hole N' the Rock. A golfer made from smashed rearview mirrors lifted a club, ready to swing. A huge bison built out of rusted metal stood ready to charge. There was even a fake "Mater" somebody made out of an old tow truck, grinning at the world. And there was a lot more stuff like that. You know. Art.

The path I followed brought me straight to the graves. I groaned. My great-grandparents had never really left Hole N' the Rock. Albert and Gladys were buried right outside their old cave-house. Their markers were carved into the wall. White gravel covered the ground over their graves. Humiliation filled my entire body. Why did my family have to be so weird?

A van pulled into the parking lot and kids spilled out, all dressed in shorts, t-shirts, and hiking boots. And I recognized some of them. Karina, Boyce, Todd, Shailene—they were kids from my school!

I ducked. I could *not* be seen here. Luckily for me, nobody saw me dodge behind a metal lion. They all sprayed on sunscreen and then headed for some hiking trails that started in the trees behind the parking lot. My whole body slumped in relief.

Sitting cross-legged on the dirt behind the sculpture, I tried to think. How was I going to get out of working here? It would be so humiliating if anyone I knew found out I did. And it would be humiliating times infinity if they found out my great-grandparents had created this place!

But I had no idea. I couldn't fake illness for more than, like, a day. What else was there for me to do? Sighing, I gave up and went inside the souvenir shop after making sure there wasn't anyone in the parking lot I recognized. As the cooler air hit my skin, a tour guide's voice hit my ears. Her words were loud and clear because Great-Grandpa's dumb cave-house was just on the other side of swinging doors by the cash register.

Those doors looked exactly like the entrance to some wild west saloon, like you see on TV. But instead of a room filled with cowboys, once you pushed through to the other side you ended up inside a mint-green kitchen. Mom said painting your kitchen this way was cool once. Like, a long, long time ago.

"Albert had many hobbies," the tour guide said from another room. "He was a painter, a sculptor, and even a taxidermist."

I rolled my eyes. Great-Grandpa Albert had had the nerve to stuff his poor pet donkey, and *then* had put him on display in his cave living room. I called the sad guy "Zombie Donkey." There were others like him in the cave-house, including a horse and a bull. This place was practically as bad as Dad's shop.

Holding my breath, I peeked over the top of the swinging doors and into the kitchen. Great-Grandma Gladys's cat clock ticked away the seconds by swinging its tail. Her ugly orange dishes were still inside her cabinets. Her tiny refrigerator hummed. But at least nobody was there. I licked dry lips, ducked under the wide space beneath the doors so I wouldn't make any noise, and tiptoed to the sink for a drink.

I turned the knob on the tap. A hissing sound came first, and then a thin stream of water trickled from the faucet. Cupping my hands to catch some, I took a sip of the lukewarm water that tasted like metal. My lips curled and I wrinkled my nose and spat it back out.

Dad's loud voice came from farther in the cave-house as he described how his Grandma Gladys had carved a deep bathtub for herself.

I should have just gone back through the swinging doors, but I decided to take a quick look around the corner to find out if the tour was almost done. Which was a mistake.

"Lizza!" Dad called. He grinned at me from the living room, where a bunch of old people in matching blue t-shirts stood admiring Zombie Donkey. "Come join us."

Every face turned to me. I ducked my head and shuffled away from the kitchen, taking my time to inch closer to the group. At least there wasn't anyone I knew inside the cave. It was only a bunch of ancient people with canes and walkers who were all wearing socks with sandals.

I hung around the back of the group. The tour guide, a lumpy woman with crinkly tanned skin whose name tag read "Cindi," did her routine in a singsong voice. Mom kept a tight hold on Dore's hand, because he kept trying to touch everything. I got tired of listening to stories about my strange family's strange house and edged away until I could sit on a flowery chair in the living room. Which was another mistake.

"You can't sit there," the tour guide said.

"But—"

"Get off that chair." The woman scowled at me and made shooing motions with her hands. All the blue-shirts in the tour group looked at me.

"Fine." I jumped to my feet.

"It's okay," Dad said, smiling at us. "She actually has a right to sit in the chair if she wants to."

"No, forget it," I blurted. "I'm going to the car."

"In a minute, Lizza," Dad said, with a slight frown. "I want to tell these folks about your special connection to this place."

I froze like one of Dad's taxidermized animals.

Tea and crumpets! He was going to blab the truth to all these people! Without thinking, I bailed. I took a shortcut by jumping over a little wire fence blocking off a bedroom filled with the frilly dolls my great-grandmother used to collect. And when he saw me, Dore yanked his arm away from Mom and followed. He crawled up onto the big fluffy bed, knocking a bunch of porcelain dolls to the cave floor. Everyone heard the *crunch*, and several people gasped.

"Those dolls are antiques." The tour guide covered her mouth with her hand.

The blue-shirts thanked Dad for the tour and shuffled back to the souvenir shop. Cindi glared at me and marched after them. And then Dad, Mom, and I listened while some of them asked for their money back.

"It wasn't a very nice tour," one old guy said in a loud voice. "We didn't even get to see that big carved bathtub."

Mom shook her head and pinched the bridge of her nose the way she does when her head hurts. Dad ran a hand over what hair was left on his head. My little brother giggled and reached for another doll.

"Sorry." I bent down to pick up one of the fallen dolls. A loud "pop" sounded and I froze, blinking at the sudden darkness that surrounded me. Was I going blind?

Dore screamed. With a hammering heart, I held my hands out in front of me and moved toward him, crunching on broken dolls with each step until I touched his curly hair. Pulling him close, I wrapped my arms around my quivering little brother.

"It's okay," I whispered. "I'm here." This time when I glanced around, my eyes had adjusted enough to make out vague shapes in the darkness. At least we weren't trapped inside the inky blackness of a deep cave with no light at all. Thanks to the small windows Grandpa Albert had added to the front of his rocky house, a tiny bit of weak sunshine made its way through the dirty glass and dusty lace curtains.

"What in the world?" Dad said. "Cindi!" he shouted. "What happened to the lights?"

After stumbling around in the dark, banging into things, and swearing a couple of times, Dad made it to the shop. Mom made her way into the bedroom and found me and Dore. Crunching across the floor as we stepped on even more dolls, we all crept out into the shop.

Cindi and Dad shined a flashlight on a panel in the wall, messing around with switches. Dad muttered under his breath.

"The wiring *is* really old," Cindi said.

Mom, Dore, and I went outside, blinking in the sudden brightness.

"Lizza," Mom said.

"I'm sorry," I blurted. "But it wasn't my fault."

Mom sighed and brushed some of my hair away from my face. She looked at me with tired eyes.

"Make the best of it, okay?" she finally said. "This place means a lot to your dad."

I didn't answer, so after shaking her head at me, Mom headed for our Explorer. I followed her and got in, leaning into the air blowing from the AC. Dore whimpered and climbed onto Mom's lap.

Dad got in, red in the face and mumbling under his breath. "Everything needs to be fixed. The plumbing, the wiring, heck—all of it."

Mom squeezed his arm. "It'll take some work, but we'll get it done."

Putting the Explorer into gear, Dad drove us out of the parking lot. I ducked down just in time, since the kids from school were getting back into their van and they looked in our direction.

As he drove, Dad talked about circuits and a leaking cistern, and then he grumbled about losing business.

"We can't lead tours in the dark. The wiring needs to be in good working condition or this business won't fly. I can't believe Roger let things get this bad."

If I were a cartoon, a giant light bulb would have appeared over my head at that second, with the word "idea" written on it. Hole N' the Rock was a tacky tourist trap that was also old and run down. It would probably take a ton of money to fix everything that needed to be fixed. And wasn't money tight?

"Money's tight," Dad said right at that second. Sometimes I swore the guy was psychic.

I tapped my finger on my chin. Dad just needed to

decide we couldn't possibly handle this business after all. It was too much hassle and too expensive to run. And once he did that, problem solved! No more cave-houses in my life.

But where to start? I sat back with a frown. How was I going to manage this?

The cave-house made me almost forget about the torn-up sign. But at five o'clock my dad got a phone call.

"No, I haven't seen my sign. It's *ruined?* Be right there." He grabbed his keys and rushed outside into the warm night.

"Oh, no," Mom said, as the door banged shut. The corners of her mouth drooped. "Just what we needed." She sighed as she fiddled with the knob on the slightly-too-large swamp cooler jammed into the window by the front door.

Guilt slammed into me. The room suddenly got way hotter, even though Mom had turned the cooler on full blast.

"I'm so sorry," I blurted. When Mom's questioning eyes hit me, I gulped and said, "I mean, Dad looked really upset. That's too bad." Mom studied me for a few long seconds before glancing away with a sigh.

"We used the credit card to pay for the billboard," she said in a soft voice, turning back to her computer.

Swallowing hard, I bit my lip. I opened my mouth to confess. Mom and Dad would understand that it was an accident, wouldn't they?

But I snapped my mouth shut. My parents might understand. But then they'd want to know what I'd been doing out there in the first place. I sat on the couch and hugged my knees to my chest. I didn't just visit Dad's billboard. I'd brought along a can of spray paint and a Sharpie. Oh, and a ladder.

Oh, *bug* snot! The ladder! I'd forgotten all about it because of that stupid cave-house.

I bolted to my feet.

"Brooklyn invited me for dinner," I blurted. "I almost forgot. I need to go."

"Oh," Mom swiveled around in her office chair. "You didn't tell me. I have a lot to do so I need you to watch Dore." Grabbing the house phone from her desk, Mom started dialing. "I'll call the Hendersons. Maybe Brooklyn can come over here."

"No." I reached for the phone, but at that moment Dore burst in and smacked into my legs. He was naked again. He grabbed the remote and turned on the TV, plopped down with a yawn, and pulled a wad of cottony stuffing from one of the holes in the couch.

"Oh, Dore." Mom dropped the phone and grabbed a pair of shorts from the floor. "You call Brooklyn, okay Lizza?"

While Mom wrangled clothes onto my brother, I took the phone into the kitchen and made a quick call to my friend's house. Nobody answered.

Grabbing some grapes from the fridge, I went out to the back steps to think. What was I going to do? I jumped a little as rustling noises came from the nearby garbage can. A small raccoon nosed around the grass nearby. He was only about the size of a small cat, and as cute as could be.

I knelt down, whispered, "You hungry?" and held out a grape. He stood on his hind legs and stared with black-ringed eyes. He stretched out his tiny head, his nose quivering. I didn't breathe. If I held completely still, maybe, just *maybe,* he'd take the food from my hand. The door banged open as Mom poked her head outside. The raccoon vanished through a hole in the fence.

"Aw, you scared it away," I said, standing up.

Mom put one hand on her hip. "Don't you remember? No more rescued animals this summer."

"I was only giving it a little treat."

"Well, what was it this time?" Mom held the door open for me, shooing me inside. "Another injured bird?"

"A raccoon."

Mom sighed. "No more treats if you see it again. Raccoons are not pets and they do not need rescuing. They destroy everything. Besides, you could get rabies if you're bitten." She stared into my eyes with her serious Mom Look, so I ducked my head.

"Fine," I mumbled. Mom laughed and kissed the top of my head.

"So is Brooklyn coming over?" she asked, taking a package of tofu from the fridge. "How about I make some adobo?"

"Um, she couldn't come," I said. "But you know I love adobo."

Worry over that stupid ladder came rushing back. How was I going to return it to Tona's garage now?

I'll just have to sneak out tonight and get it.

Turning my back so my mother wouldn't read the guilt all over my face, I started to clear some of her books and notes off the table. One scrap of paper had three lines scribbled on it—one of Mom's haikus. I smiled and picked up the paper to read out loud:

"We just bought a cave.
Plumbing and wiring are old.

What do we do now?"

"That's a good one," I said. "Can you write another?"

"No." Mom snatched the paper from me and tossed it into the garbage. "And don't tell your dad, okay?" I smiled and she grinned and smoothed my hair.

"I was just thinking about all the repairs on the cave we'll have to do. But I don't want Clint to feel bad. He's got enough to worry about," Mom added. She grabbed a knife and sliced an onion. "Anyway, I should write *real* haikus. Remember what I told you? Haikus are supposed to create images of nature or the seasons." She set a frying pan on the stove and turned the burner on. "Serious poets don't write haikus like the silly one I came up with."

I found a blank scrap of paper and a pencil. "Okay, I'm going to write one. It will be about nature. Sort of." When I finished, I read it out loud to Mom while she put rice into the steamer.

"Grandpa built a house,
With shovels and dynamite.
A hole in a rock."

Mom laughed. I did, too, but then thoughts of the oddball place we now owned, along with my little ladder problem, drained the happy right out of me. I took a deep breath. I couldn't talk to Mom about the ladder, but I could talk about the cave.

"Mom, why did Dad have to buy Hole N' the Rock?" I asked. I grabbed plates to set the table. "It's embarrassing."

"I can understand how you feel about it," Mom said. "But it's important to your dad, remember? It's part of his history, and so it's part of yours, too. Not everybody thinks it's embarrassing."

"But *I* do," I grouched.

Mom tugged a lock of my tangled hair and grinned at me. "What do I keep saying? You can't expect everyone to think the same way you do."

I folded my arms. "Yes, I can," I mumbled, picking up my pencil to write another haiku.

Mom laughed and stirred the adobo on the stove. A spicy smell filled the air, making my mouth water.

Dad burst in and I dropped my pencil.

"Look at this." He tossed his phone to Mom. I edged closer and peeked over her shoulder.

Just as I figured, there was a photo of Dad's billboard on the screen. "Crap Taxidermy" was still hilarious. A giggle burst out of my mouth.

"Oh, laugh if you want, Liz, but this isn't funny at all."

"What are you going to do?" I asked. I bit my lip so I'd stop laughing.

"I called the sheriff. He said his guys will dust the ladder they found for prints."

My jaw almost hit the floor.

Dad laughed. "Yeah, I couldn't believe it either. That dang idiot left his ladder!" He slapped his knee, laughing like a donkey. "The sheriff told me vandalism can earn someone a big fine if they're caught. And sometimes even a month or two in jail."

I went cold. I sat at the table and clenched my fists so hard my fingernails dug into my palms. Brooklyn and I had snuck the stupid ladder out of my neighbor's garage without asking, because, well, we needed a ladder but didn't want anyone to ask *why* we needed one. I'd never really thought about how hard it would be to put the ladder back. And now it was too late.

Dad called a friend while Mom put her arm around him and patted his back. And I chewed my nails.

Tona, the nicest guy ever, could end up in trouble. *Big* trouble, because of me.

The next morning went by with no news about fingerprints. I was almost too busy to worry much. Since I broke all those dumb dolls at Hole N' the Rock, my parents expected me to do any chore they gave me.

I'd just finished washing the lunch dishes and was sitting down to read when Dad walked into the living room.

"Sweep out the shop for me, Lizza," he said. "I got a request to do another dog."

"But your sign got ruined, Dad, and you already took it down. How did someone know to call you?"

"Word of mouth does wonders, kid," Dad said with a grin. "My work speaks for itself. Friends tell friends and I get more business."

I sat back and folded my arms across my chest. "Oh."

"Hurry, okay?" Dad said.

I sighed, got to my feet, and tossed my book onto the couch. At least I'd get to spend more time with Rosie. I stomped to the shop.

Rosie liked being out of her cage, so I let her wander around on Dad's work table.

"Why do people freeze-dry their dogs?" I grumbled to her while I swept. "You don't freeze dry Grandma and stick *her* on the mantel." I paused for a second. "At least I *hope* nobody does that."

Rosie waved a leg at me in agreement.

I was almost done sweeping when Brooklyn stuck her head inside the garage door.

"Hey, Lizza," she called. "Oh, hi, Rosie." She gently picked up our fuzzy friend and carried her over to a bench against the wall. This was one of the reasons Brooklyn and I were BFF's. Tarantulas didn't freak her out. She loved animals almost as much as I did.

There was a deer head on the bench next to her. Holding Rosie in one hand, Brooklyn reached out to scratch the deer between its antlers, like it was alive. Swinging her blonde braid over her shoulder, she glanced around to make sure nobody else was there before she talked again.

"Did you take Tona's ladder back?" she whispered.

I froze. "Mmm—" Guilt grew heavy in my gut. What could I say? Brooks was going to kill me!

But my friend took my weird "mmm" sound as a "yes." She sighed in relief. "Well, at least Tona has it back."

While I put the broom in the supply closet, I tried to find the right words to break the news to her about the ladder, but nothing came to me. Before I could say even one word, Brooklyn stood up and took Rosie back to her cage.

"You know, my parents would have killed me if they knew I'd helped you ruin your dad's sign."

"Yeah," I said softly. And I completely lost my nerve. I couldn't tell Brooklyn *now*. What if she never talked to me again for doing something so stupid? "If *my* parents ever find out who ruined Dad's billboard," I said, "I'll be grounded until I'm dead and for like five hundred more years after that." I hung up the dust pan. "But let's forget about it, okay?"

"Deal," Brooklyn said.

"Lizza!" my dad shouted from the back yard. "Come here." My friend and I both jumped.

"I gotta go." Brooklyn grabbed her bag and sprinted to the garage door. "Junior lifeguard training. Bye Lizza! Bye Rosie!"

My dad didn't sound mad, but I couldn't blame my bestie for bailing on me. After talking about that dumb ladder, we were both as jumpy as bank robbers who heard the sirens getting closer. Sighing, I headed to the back yard.

Dad had his cell phone to his ear. He grinned at me as I crossed our scraggly lawn.

"Somebody's sick," he said. "I need you to work this afternoon in the souvenir shop."

Cookies! I stumbled over my own feet.

"But I'm only twelve," I blurted. "Isn't that against the law?"

"Nope," Dad said, tucking his phone into his back pocket. He turned back to the picnic table and picked up a metal box that looked like a small cage. "You can stock shelves. You just can't use the cash register. The manager will handle that."

"But Dad—"

"No arguing." Dad made the "stop" gesture with his hand. "Your mom will take you. Remember all those dolls you broke? Some of them were too crushed to repair, so they're gone forever. We can save two, though, and it costs a lot to fix antique toys. You need to work to pay me and your mom back."

My eyes stung. I blinked back mad tears. I even think I growled a little as I stomped inside.

While Mom drove to Hole N' the Rock, the only noise came from the back seat where Dore watched videos on Mom's phone. Well, one video. He played the theme song from Sponge Bob over and over again, and never once stopped giggling.

When we got there, I stood in the parking lot for a while before I could make myself go inside the souvenir shop. High above me, a sculpture of Franklin Roosevelt's head stared off into nothing. Grandpa Albert had carved the guy's big, fat head above his cave-house. I'd always thought it looked like the spirit of the stone trying to come out so he could kick the butts of anyone who blasted holes in his body. Also, it looked weird. Who carves giant heads into the outside walls of their house?

Great-Grandpa Albert, that's who, my brain said in a snotty voice.

After Mom honked and waved her hand, telling me to go, I stomped inside the souvenir shop. My stomach hurt. And I couldn't get that stupid Sponge Bob song out of my head for the rest of the day.

The souvenir shop was cool and a little dark. Rows of shelves held the kind of stuff you'd expect to find in a place that sold things for tourists: along with post cards and polished rocks there were t-shirts, local maps, and cheap toys next to a stack of expensive books about the national parks around us.

The manager, a pretty woman with black hair coiled into a messy bun on top of her head, walked over.

"You're Lizza, right?" She shook my hand like I was an adult. She swept a stray strand of wavy hair out of her eyes. "I'm Zochee," she said, smiling at me. "Welcome."

She put me to work right away, stocking shelves with rolls of toilet paper. Yes, that's what I said. The rolls were wrapped in labels that had the name of an Old West movie star, John Wayne, printed on them.

I crinkled my face in confusion, but I didn't care enough to ask why we were selling this stuff. I mean, the toilet paper rolls were hardly any weirder than anything else on the shelves. Think refrigerator magnets that looked like cow skulls, salt and pepper shakers made to look like covered wagons, and rabbit's foot key chains. Poor bunnies.

From my spot inside the shop, snatches of the cave-house tour reached me. The words floated out from behind the swinging doors.

"As you can see, Albert was a talented artist," the cranky tour guide, Cindi, said.

As someone familiar with all of Great-Grandpa Albert's paintings *and* his big Dead President's Head sculpture, I wouldn't have said "talented artist." Maybe, "Somebody Who Tried Really Hard."

After a couple of hours of having to listen to Cindi, I hadn't learned anything new, other than the tour was BORING. Why did people pay money to walk around in a dusty cave-house filled with dead animals and ugly dolls? Ew.

I called Brooklyn when Zochee went outside for a few minutes. I told her where I was—Embarrassingville, USA—and what I was doing—being tortured with boredom.

"I'm dying," I whispered. "Help me!"

"Maybe you can think of a way to make things fun," Brooklyn said. "You know, turn it into a game, or something." My shoulders slumped. Sometimes, Brooklyn was way too chirpy. She must have been a Disney princess in a former life. Or Mary Poppins.

"Like what?" I grabbed a Peanut Butter Twix bar from a box by the register and stuffed half of it into my mouth.

"I don't know, but you have great ideas, Lizza," she told me, snapping her gum. "I'm sorry you're stuck working out there, but I bet you can think of a way to make it fun. I have to go, ok? I'm going shopping with Mom. Zoodles!"

"Captain Crunch," I mumbled back. With a frown, I hung up and popped the last bite of my free treat into my mouth.

"Don't eat any more candy," Zochee said, coming inside with a big box in her arms. "We'll have to write that off as a loss." She winked at me as she walked by.

"You ate some candy?" Dad said, popping through the swinging doors. I jumped. When had *he* gotten here?

"Those aren't free, you know," he said. "I'm adding the candy bar to the total you owe me." He ducked back inside the cave while I brushed chocolate crumbs off my shirt.

"Gee, thanks," I said under my breath. I couldn't even have a little snack once in a while? This stupid job was really going to kill me.

Zochee breezed back by the register, humming to herself. Her brown skin was perfect and she had a toothpaste commercial smile. She looked like she belonged in movies, not managing a roadside attraction in a tiny desert town.

"Don't worry about the candy," Zochee told me, leaning on her elbows against the counter. "Like I said, I'll write it off." She winked at me again and I grinned back at her. At least I had a friend here.

"You're so cute, Lizza," she told me. "Where does your mom come from?"

"She's from the Philippines," I said, smiling. "And thanks."

"I thought so," Zochee said. "Asian people are lovely."

"Where do you come from?" I asked. "From hearing you talk, I guess Mexico." I loved how Zochee said my name, making it sound like "Leeza."

"You got it, sweetie," she told me with a big smile.

"I've never heard a name like yours before, though," I told her.

Smiling, Zochee grabbed a slip of paper and wrote 'Xochitl.' "This is how my name is really spelled," she said. "It's pronounced "Socheel."

I repeated her name. "I like it," I said. "But why do you spell it wrong on your name tag?"

Zochee laughed. "It's a joke between me and my boyfriend," she said. "I first met him at the post office. He was behind me as we stood in line. He saw my name on a letter and tried to say it. I told him the right way to pronounce it, but 'Zochee' was the best he could do. It became his nickname for me."

"And you like it?" I asked.

"I love it," Zochee said. "My boyfriend is the most wonderful man. He's why I decided to stay in Moab for a while."

"And work *here*?" I asked.

Zochee laughed again. "I like this place. It's unusual and fun. Even a little eccentric. Like Albert and Gladys were."

I had no answer I would dare say out loud, because I would replace the word "eccentric" with bizarro. Or cringy.

Reading my face, Zochee giggled. "I heard once that Gladys used to love bubble baths so much, she'd stay in her rock bathtub all day. Friends who came to visit would sit in the living room and chat while she talked to them from her bathroom."

Ugh! I stuck out my tongue and made a gagging sound.

"Cheer up, Lizza. I bet you'll learn to love this place," Zochee said.

That afternoon was the longest one I could ever remember. The minutes crawled by about as fast as a giant sloth. I hung plastic jewelry on hooks, coiled fake snakes on shelves, and stacked even more rolls of John Wayne toilet paper. I wanted to die of humiliation. And then, somehow, I knocked over a box on a shelf above the register. A bunch of snow globes with scorpions inside fell on the cash register and rolled everywhere. The register began making funny sounds, and Zochee couldn't figure out what was wrong, so she asked Dad to look at it.

"How'd those keys get stuck?" Dad scowled. My face burned while I scrambled around, picking up the snow globes. Did I mention they had scorpions inside? Why?

Zochee told him about the falling snow globes. Dad squinted his eyes at me. After fiddling around with the cash register for a few minutes, he got it working right again. By that time, I was out of sight behind a row of shelves as I unpacked a crate of stuffed pink pigs. Dad must have forgotten I was there, because he said, "If she keeps this up, I can't have her work here anymore. I need things to run smoothly."

Yes! I stuck a hand over my mouth to keep from yelling as a lightning bolt of happiness shot through me. Dad would fire me if I kept screwing up! Problem solved. I could go back to pretending I had nothing to do with this place.

Thoughts popped and fizzed in my brain. What could I do that would be, well, just annoying enough to make my dad want to fire me?

I picked up a handmade ceramic bowl. If I dropped a box of these, Dad would fire me for sure. I bit my lip. I didn't want to break a bunch of stuff, especially after tearing up my dad's sign *and* breaking those dolls. I put the bowl back on the shelf and glanced around. What else could I do?

Nothing came to me until Zochee told me to get a dust pan from the supply closet. There was an old pair of swim fins stuck on a high shelf, along with a snorkeling mask. I got a brilliant idea. An *epic* idea!

Bingo! I'd put on a little show. I'd get in the way and mess up the tours. Dad would fire me for sure. I grinned.

After telling Zochee I needed a pee break, I snuck into

the cave-house while Dad was busy at the far end, leading another tour. I tiptoed inside the big bathroom, the one with the hand-carved bathtub. Dad had decided to fill it with water and a bunch of bubbles, I guess in honor of his dead grandma. I stuck the swim fins on my feet and swung my legs over the side. The water was way less than warm, but I gritted my teeth and forced myself to duck down inside the tub. I winced as the cold water soaked into my shorts and t-shirt. Then I put on the mask.

The tour group got close to the bathroom. Smiling, I held my breath. Peeking up over the edge of the tall tub, I watched and waited. The moment the door cracked open, I jumped to my feet and made a giant splash. But when I tried to swing my legs up and over the side of the tub, those frog feet got caught. With a scream, I fell and landed in a soggy heap on the floor while a crowd gathered around the bathroom doorway.

"Whoa," I got up, pulled off my mask and stared at all the tourists who were gawking at me like I was a ghost. "Where am I? I was snorkeling in Australia, and suddenly I got sucked into this big whirlpool! *I thought I was a goner,*" I said in a loud whisper. "Now I'm in some weird cave."

The crowd giggled a little while Dad shoved his way over to me. His face was not happy in any way you could imagine.

"What are you *doing?*" he said. "Get out of here!"

"But where am I?" I stumbled forward in my froggy swim fins, lifting my feet high and making loud, squelching noises with every step. People backed away. "Wait, I know," I said. "I found the lost city of Atlantis!"

An older couple applauded, and after throwing one another confused looks, the rest of the tourists clapped, too. And suddenly everybody laughed. My jaw hung open.

"This tour is more entertaining than it used to be," the old guy said. "Well done!"

Dad's face, red as a boiled beet, lost its angry look. He laughed weakly. "Thanks," he said. "We do try to entertain."

Rumpelstiltskin! My epic plan obviously didn't work. Steaming on the inside and dripping wet on the outside, I left the bathroom, walking like a demented frog. The tourists kept clapping.

Zochee, who'd come in to see what the noise was about, handed me a towel.

"What a cute idea, Lizza!" she said. "But next time, wear a swimsuit."

Bathtub snorkeling:
I thought Dad would send me home.
But no. He didn't.

I had to work again the next day. I stocked more shelves, and then Zochee introduced me to Doug, the maintenance man. He was young-ish, maybe only out of high school for a few years. His head was shaved, he had a nose ring and his skin was the deep tan of someone who lived in the sun. And he was wearing a t-shirt that said "Save the spotted owls." Which made me like him. At least a little.

"I need some help outside," Doug told me. "Are you afraid of heights?"

"No way," I said. "I go climbing all the time."

I followed Doug outside into the bright sunlight. When my eyes adjusted, I scanned the parking lot to make sure there wasn't anyone who might know me. There was a family with little kids posing for photos with the old "Mater" truck, but nobody I knew. Whew.

"You see Roosevelt?" Doug pointed to the giant sculpted head in the wall above the cave-house, like I'd never noticed it before.

"Uh huh." I scratched at a bug bite on my arm.

"See how his nostrils are white, while the rest of the sculpture is the same red color as the stone?" Doug asked.

"You can't *not* see that." I wrinkled up my face. "We're looking right up his nose."

"They're discolored because hard water pools there when it rains. Your dad doesn't like how it looks."

I laughed. "It does look kind of funny."

Doug shrugged. "I guess." Then he pointed to a huge ladder propped up against the front of my great-grandparents' cave-house. It reached almost to the top of the rock and stood next to Roosevelt's head. There were also some long ropes nearby, attached to metal rings hammered into the sandstone formation that Gladys and Albert had called home.

"Hey, why the ropes?" I asked.

"Albert built a platform to stand on when he carved Roosevelt, but he used ropes, too, for safety. He's the one who put those rings there to tether the rope."

Doug handed me a safety harness.

"Your dad asked me to clean off those white mineral deposits, but an electrician's coming to look at the wiring today. I need to be around for him, so I figured you could do the first job in my place."

I'm being asked to clean out the nose holes of a carving of President Roosevelt, I thought to myself. *I should be getting paid for this. A lot.*

While I put on the harness, Doug made sure the ladder was on steady ground so it wouldn't move. Then, he helped me get tethered to the safety rope. I glanced around one more time to make sure nobody was watching.

Doug handed me a scrub brush with sharp wire bristles, a bottle of cleaner, and some yellow rubber gloves, along with what looked like a pair of thick, nerdy glasses with an elastic band that held them in place.

"This has acid in it," he said, pointing to the bottle. "Be careful and use the gloves and these safety goggles."

With a gulp, I yanked the gloves on and shoved the goggles onto my face.

"Squirt some of this on the rock, wait a few seconds, and then scrub," Doug said. Then, he walked away. With a scowl, I climbed up about twenty feet to where Roosevelt was, struggling to keep hold of the bottle and the brush while I moved up the rungs. Wobbling, I nearly lost my footing.

I held my breath and slowed down as I continued to climb. What was it about me and ladders? They sure popped up in my life a lot, for some reason. I smiled to myself. At least this time, if I fell, I'd be saved by the rope.

From up here, Roosevelt's head was huge and so was his nose. I sprayed some cleaner into the whopping nostril closest to me and waited. It took most of the bottle of cleaner to cover that one majorly big nose hole. Finally, I started scrubbing. And scrubbing.

Nothing came off. The white nostril looked just as white as it had before I'd begun. The sun climbed higher, the air got hotter, and sweat trickled down the back of my neck.

"Hey, Lizza!" somebody shouted. "What are you doing?"

I looked down, and froze. Below me, Tona stood in the cactus garden.

Spit! I cursed in my head. "Just cleaning," I called.

Even from twenty feet in the air, I could hear Tona's chuckle. I'd have been kind of mad if I hadn't also been totally guilty of taking his ladder without asking. And, if I wasn't so afraid everybody would find out I'd ruined my dad's sign.

"What are you doing here?" I moved down a few rungs. Since the cleaner didn't work, I wasn't going to stand there all day on the ladder in front of all those tourists. More and more people were pulling into the parking lot, and lots of them were pointing at me.

But before Tona answered, somebody shouted, "Hey, look at that kid on the ladder!" My face burned and I started climbing down the rungs as fast as I could.

"Be careful, Lizza," Tona called. "Do you need some help?"

I was about halfway to the ground by then, so I dropped the bottle and brush into the cactus.

"No," I said. "I'm fine."

But apparently the tourists didn't think so, because by then, a pretty big group had gathered in front of the cactus garden.

"She's going to fall," a man said.

"That kid shouldn't be up there," a woman said.

"Little girl, you get down from there," a quivery old-person's voice said.

Little girl? That did it. I *had* to show them I knew what I was doing. So, when I was only about ten feet up, I moved to the side of the ladder, ready to rappel the last few feet to the ground. I'd learned how to rappel last summer during climbing lessons. It was fun and easy—you lowered yourself little by little using the rope attached to a special hook on your harness. I'd bow for the tourists once I reached the ground. Ha.

I jumped to the side, expecting the rope to hold me in place. It didn't. I'd forgotten these ropes weren't set up for rappelling, they were safety ropes. These ropes were set up to catch me, *after* I first fell about three feet.

For a second or two, my stomach tried to climb out of my throat as I zoomed a few feet lower. Somebody screamed—it might have been me. The sudden jerk as the rope stopped my free fall made me let go of it. And then I tipped upside down, dangling like a pathetic human puppet controlled by an invisible giant.

Tona scrambled up the ladder and grabbed me. He got me turned right side up and swung me toward him so I could get my feet on the rungs. Shaking, I climbed back to the ground, while the tourists clapped.

"You're a hero," the old lady said to Tona. "And you, young lady, need to stay off ladders."

My face burned like lava while I wriggled out of my harness and ran inside to hide. In the green kitchen, I sat at the table and made up a haiku.

> *Giant president,*
> *Your boogery nose is gross.*
> *But I won't pick it.*

It didn't make me feel any better. The only comforting thought was how Dad would fire me after he learned what had happened. But he didn't.

"You better keep off ladders from now on. I'll have you lead the tours," Dad told me.

When we got home, I sat on the back steps. Bits of stringy white fluff from our cottonwood trees floated by on the hot breeze. Scratching at a scab on my knee, I ducked my head and closed my eyes.

Corn nuts! I told myself. I was actually good at climbing and rappelling. I'd taken lessons for, well, forever! How could I have done what I did today?

I let out a long sigh. At least Zochee had let me call Mom to get an early ride home.

Something moved by the back fence and I glanced up. The little raccoon who'd been there earlier inched along the peeling boards, sniffing as it headed toward a metal box. What was that thing? I leaned forward to get a better look and gasped. It was a trap Dad had put out to catch this little creature. I jumped up and shouted, waving my arms. But I was too late.

The little raccoon had already darted its paw inside for whatever treat was in there, and now it was caught in the trap. Quivering, it looked up at me with terror in its tiny face.

I clapped a hand over my mouth. What could I do? I whirled to see if anyone was around. Luckily, Mom had gone to the store with my little brother and Dad was inside the garage. That was easy to figure out because through the open door, Clint Brown's voice sang about

Texas or cows or something. Dad hummed along, probably while sticking glass eyeballs into the empty sockets of dead deer.

I hurried inside to grab a towel from the bathroom. Once I was back in the yard, I tiptoed over to the raccoon.

"It's okay," I whispered. I kept my movements slow and my voice soft. "I won't hurt you." When I got close enough, I tossed the towel onto the animal and grabbed it, towel and trap and all. Then I snuck it inside my room and put the bundle on the bed. After making a quick dash to the kitchen for the house phone, I returned and closed the door.

I dialed the number of the local Humane Society. Evan, the manager, answered.

"Hey, Lizza. Checking on Gary? He's doing great."

"Thanks, but I need your help." I told him what had happened. After I described the trap, he told me how to spring it. Keeping the phone tucked against my ear, I followed Evan's directions. After a few failed tries, I pressed a lever and the trap finally opened. The raccoon yanked out its paw and darted to the floor. With nowhere to go, it finally curled up on my rug and licked its paw.

"It worked," I told Evan. Relief made my whole body light. "Thanks."

"Tell me about the raccoon," he said. "How big?"

"Maybe the size of a small cat," I said.

"Likely a female, then," Evan said. "Hard to tell with raccoons. Is its paw or leg broken?"

"I don't think so," I said. "She ran around my room a few times. But now she's licking her paw."

"Then her paw's likely hurt. Even if nothing's broken, the injury means she might not be able to survive in the wild. I'd love to take her if you can get her over to my place in town."

"No," I said, watching the little animal. "I'll take care of her."

"You sure?"

"Yes." I ignored the tiny voice in my brain saying, *Wait a second, there, Liz.* "Thank you *so* much for helping me." I hung up.

My mind raced. What the holy heck was I going to do with the raccoon? I'd promised Mom no more rescues this summer. No matter how much I begged, all I'd get from her would be a big, giant *no*. At that moment, the grinding gears of the garbage truck rumbling toward my house gave me an idea. Mrs. Baker down the street had an old dog carrier her ancient Chihuahua used to sleep in before it had died. She'd stuck it out on the curb this morning since today was garbage day.

I sprinted to the street and grabbed the carrier just in time before the garbage truck hissed to a stop in front of Mrs. Baker's house. I brought the carrier inside and put it on my bed.

Before you could say "rascally raccoon," my new friend was inside the Chihuahua's old carrier, eating grapes and carrots and drinking water from a tiny metal dish. She curled up, licking her injured paw, and soon, she closed her eyes. I shoved old shoes on the floor of my closet to the side and put the carrier in there.

"You won't be stuck here forever," I whispered to her. "I'll let you out whenever I'm in my room. Just don't let my parents see you." I eased the closet door closed.

I stood with my hands on my hips and smiled. I'd managed this situation pretty well. This gave me, like, a million warm fuzzies. And after my totally humiliating morning at work, I needed *something* to go right.

"Lizza? Where are you?" Dad called from the front

yard. I went outside with a bubble of lemony sunshine glowing inside my chest.

My dad wasn't alone. A man in a sheriff's uniform stood on our porch. Dad stood next to him with his arms folded across his chest.

Pop. Goodbye sunshine bubble.

"Where's your mom?" Dad asked me.

"She went to the store," I said, pulling at a loose thread on my t-shirt.

"Oh." Dad turned back to the guy in the uniform.

"So, like I said, that guy called us yesterday," the sheriff said. "We shared a photo of the ladder online, asking if anyone recognized it since it had such an odd paint job. We didn't think it would help, but the young man happened to see it. Says the ladder's his and it went missing from his garage last week."

I backed inside the house. Closing the front door softly behind me, I tried to breathe while my heart tried to force its way out of my chest. Tona's ladder *was* unusual. After all, it was pink. Tona had told me how he let his niece paint it one summer when she visited, just to keep the kid busy and out of his hair.

I'm toast, I told myself. *Crud muffins.*

I hid in my room, waiting for someone to come and arrest me. No one did, so after about five minutes of pacing and chewing off my fingernails, I grabbed a pen and an old school notebook and forced myself to sit. I didn't plan to write a confession, but it happened. As a haiku.

I took the ladder,

> *Borrowed from Tona, my friend,*
> *To ruin Dad's sign.*

I tore out the page, crumpled it and shoved it under my bed so it could join my single socks and dust bunnies. Wasn't *somebody* going to come for me? Taking a deep breath, I dared to peek out from my room. The hallway was empty. I crept into the front room and glanced out the window. The sheriff was gone.

My shoulders sagged with relief, and suddenly, my stomach rumbled, reminding me how empty it was. When I went into the kitchen, Mom was back and reading at the table while Dad stood at the stove, dumping a can of tomato sauce into a pot. Another pot, filled with water, simmered on the stove, and a box of spaghetti waited on the counter.

When my dad saw me, he grinned. "I'm sure they're going to get the guy who ruined my billboard," he said. "I can feel it."

"You don't really think Tona's the guy who did it, do you?" My torn fingernails hurt, and I winced and shoved my hands into the back pockets of my jeans to hide my fingertips.

Dad's eyebrows shot up. "How did you know it was Tona's ladder?"

Mom looked up from her book.

The water bubbled as it started to boil. I swallowed, hard. "I heard the sheriff describe the ladder."

Mom looked back down at her book.

Moldy mildew! I cursed to myself. I really had to be more careful!

"Oh, I don't think Tona did it. Of course not," Dad said, dumping the spaghetti into the pot. "He needs to lock his garage, though. The police are questioning the neighbors. Somebody's got to have seen something."

Old Mr. Stricker came to mind. He'd been mowing his lawn when he saw me on my bike right after I'd ruined Dad's sign. Why did he have to do yard work so early in the morning on that particular day? Had the sheriff already talked to him? I excused myself, sprinted back to my bedroom, fished out my haiku confession, and snuck into the bathroom to flush it down the toilet.

At dinner, I couldn't eat. My spaghetti looked like a pile of red worms on the plate. Mom and Dad talked softly. Dore slurped his nutrition shake. Then Mom's phone buzzed, and her face lit up like it did whenever she saw a number from the Philippines.

She answered, speaking in rapid Tagalog. I didn't pay much attention until Mom's face crumpled and she began to sob.

When she could finally talk, she told us what had happened. A couple of hours ago, my grandma, *Lola* Marita, had had a heart attack. She'd been taken to the hospital. That was all they knew.

The next few hours were crazy. Mom threw random items into her suitcase, like a pair of nail clippers or a single shoe. Then she'd just plop down on the couch and cry. Dad made tons of phone calls and got online to figure out plane tickets.

Our elderly neighbor, Mrs. Stricker—the other half of the nosy neighbor brigade—came over to say we were watering our lawn too much and flooding her yard. The lumpy woman's wrinkly face was set in its permanent frown until she heard our news and saw the craziness. Her expression changed into one of concern.

"Let me help," she said, already halfway to the kitchen.

By nine o'clock, Mom had a suitcase packed full of clothing, a carry-on filled with snacks and magazines, and a ride to Salt Lake City, thanks to Mr. Stricker. From there, she'd fly to the Philippines. Her trip would probably take her at least twenty-four hours.

When Mom kissed me goodbye about ten that night, ready to get into Mr. Stricker's car, I couldn't help crying. Dore clung to her and sobbed until Dad picked him up.

"It'll be okay, babe," Dad whispered to Mom, kissing her on the cheek. Mom wrapped her arms around his neck.

"Dore is almost out of ketchup," she said in a cracked voice. "And go easy on Lizza, okay?"

We all hugged, and Mom whispered, "*Mahal na mahal kita*. I love you very much." Dad and I whispered it back. Dore kept crying.

That night, I didn't fall asleep for a long time. The raccoon kept rustling the newspaper I'd put in her carrier. I finally got up and took her out. Huddled on the floor next to a pile of worn-out stuffed animals, I held my real-live animal friend on my lap and stroked her soft fur.

"You need a name, don't you?" I asked her. Thinking a minute, I decided on one. "I'll call you Chewie," I whispered to the raccoon. "Okay?" Her cute furry face didn't really look like Chewbacca from Star Wars, but she liked to chew on everything.

Finding a perfect name for my new friend gave me a teensy warm fuzzy, but it went away fast. What was going to happen to my *lola?* What if she died? My stomach twisted itself and I went cold inside. I started to breathe faster and a tear ran down my face. The tiny woman I'd only met once in person was still a big part of my life. We talked during video chats every week, and her laugh was one of my favorite things in the world. She always thought everything I said was so funny.

Chewie closed her eyes and her little warm body helped my breathing slow to normal. I finally fell asleep inside my closet by about the time the neighbor's chickens were waking up.

About ten-thirty the next morning, I jumped awake. Loud thumping sounds came from somewhere in the house. Digging gunk out of the corners of my eyes, I stumbled to my feet. Chewie was asleep on my bed, so I left her there, making sure to close my door.

My little brother was in the kitchen, hanging onto pantry shelves about halfway up to the ceiling. He'd knocked things to the floor as he climbed.

"Come on." I grabbed him around the waist and lifted him down. "You're not supposed to do that. Let's pick this up." But Dore squealed and ran out of the room. Shoving tangled hair out of my eyes, I bent down to pick up cans of chili and bags of rice.

Dad popped his head in the kitchen. "You're finally up," he said. "Keep an eye on your brother. I've got to work in the shop."

"How's Mom?" I asked.

"She's about halfway there." He pressed his lips into something that was probably supposed to be a grin, but wasn't. And then he ducked back outside.

Dore clamped his lips shut and shook his head when I gave him a nutrition shake. He also kept taking all his clothes off. I got him into an old pair of shorts when the doorbell rang, but he took them off the second my back was turned. Luckily, it was Brooklyn on our front porch.

"I heard," she said, giving me a hug with one arm and balancing a foil-covered dish with the other. "This is from my mom. She figured you guys might like help with meals while your mom's gone. It's chicken and rice but the 'chicken' is soy. Can I hang out here, today?"

My eyes stung. "Yeah. Thanks."

We stuck Heidi's casserole in the fridge and then my friend helped me clean up the kitchen. I got Dore wrapped in his orange blanket and he curled up under the kitchen table.

"Get ready to answer the door," Brooklyn told me. "Mom told the ladies at our church about you guys. They're bringing more food."

I gulped. "Wow, thanks."

After we got the kitchen in order, we tried to coax Dore out from under the table by offering to play Candyland, but he just whimpered and closed his eyes.

The rest of the morning, the doorbell rang every few minutes, and both neighbors and strangers appeared on our porch. Each one of them had something foil-covered or plastic-wrapped or sealed in Tupperware to hand me. They all said they hoped my grandma would be okay. I said "thanks" and blinked back tears. Soon, our fridge was jammed full and the table and counters were loaded with brownies, cookies, and even some kind of dessert with gummy worms sticking out of it.

Dore kept grabbing my hand and taking me to the kitchen, but he wouldn't eat any bananas. And we were out of Cheetos. He cried for a long time when I told him there weren't any.

"I don't know what to do," I told Brooklyn. "He's never been like this."

Dad walked in then and blinked at the sight of food all over the place.

"People from Brooklyn's church brought it," I said.

Dad crossed the room and put an arm around my friend. "Tell them all thanks, okay?" he said in a rough voice, giving her a quick hug.

She smiled. "Sure."

My father cleared his throat, swiped a hand over his eyes and grabbed a plate. He loaded it with taco salad, grabbed several cookies, and then turned to leave.

"Dad, we really need to get some Cheetos. Can you go to the store?" I asked him.

"Not now," Dad said with a frown. He spotted Dore curled up under the table and the lines carved between his eyebrows deepened.

"Take care of your little brother, okay? This is hard on him."

"But Dad, he needs Cheetos!"

"Give him a banana or one of his shakes," Dad said in a grouchy voice. He grabbed a Pepsi from the fridge, pushed open the door with his elbow, and took his lunch to the shop.

I scowled at the back door. Brooklyn squeezed my arm and handed me a cookie.

"Let's get your brother out from under the table," she said.

It took us nearly an hour, but Brooklyn and I finally got Dore to come out from his hiding place. We wrapped him in his blanket and put him on the couch to watch cartoons. He still refused to eat anything.

With a tired huff, Brooklyn plopped onto the sofa while I wrapped my arms around my little brother, wishing again he could talk. He missed Mom and so did I. This wasn't working. How was I supposed to take care of him? How did Mom do it?

Heidi picked Brooklyn up at two o'clock to take her to swimming lessons. My bestie hugged me before she left. "I'll call tomorrow," she said. "Tater tots."

Glancing down at Dore, I said: "Ketchup."

I was about to curl up on the couch when the doorbell rang. My brother stirred and whimpered.

"It's okay," I whispered to him, kissing his forehead. "Probably somebody else bringing food."

I stumbled to the door. "Well, whoever you are, I hope you brought Cheetos," I mumbled.

But when I opened our front door, Mrs. Barlow was on the porch. She didn't have any Cheetos.

"Oh, crap," I said. "Uh, I mean..."

Mrs. Barlow's pale face flushed pink. "Well, that's quite a welcome."

"I'm sorry," I said, wishing I could pull my t-shirt over my face to hide my blush. "It's been a long day."

"Is your mom home?" the teacher asked.

"No." I edged outside so I was standing on the porch with the woman. Her "talking voice" was kind of like my "yelling voice," and Dore really needed his sleep.

"Is your dad here, then?" she asked.

Before I could answer, Dore popped outside. Ketchup dripped down his chest and arms and tears streamed down his face.

"My goodness," Mrs. Barlow gasped. She dropped her purse.

"Oh, Dore," I said with a sigh. "He's not hurt," I told the teacher, taking my brother's hand. "It's not blood. It's ketchup. He must have tried to get the cap off himself."

Mrs. Barlow came inside without asking and helped

me get Dore cleaned off. After we wiped the sticky red stuff away, I had him sit at the table while I sliced bananas and squirted ketchup on a plate. I held my breath, but Dore popped a banana slice into his mouth the second I put the plate in front of him. I slumped into a chair and yawned.

"*Finally,*" I said. "He hasn't eaten anything yet today."

Mrs. Barlow's forehead crinkled. "Oh dear," she said. "Do you have any cucumbers?"

"What?" What kind of question was that? Did she want me to make her a salad? "Uh, yeah," I said. "In the fridge."

Mrs. Barlow got one, went to the sink, peeled and sliced the cucumber, and brought it over to Dore.

He grinned his dimple-showing smile, grabbed a slice, dipped it in ketchup, and ate it. My mouth hung open. Dore never touched anything but Cheetos and bananas!

"How did you do that?" I said.

"Last year we tried lots of new foods at school. He loves cucumbers and watermelon." Mrs. Barlow sat down by Dore and patted his shoulder. "We also gave him soft clothes without scratchy tags to wear at school. Then he kept his clothes on all day." She put her hand on my arm.

"You know those tests we want to do?" she asked.

I nodded, but my eyes were stuck to my little brother. I couldn't believe he was eating those cucumbers. And he'd kept his clothes on at school? That was *huge*.

"The tests are nothing scary," Mrs. Barlow said. "All they do is get Dore special help, so we can teach him to do things like eat different foods and communicate better."

"Oh," I said, still staring at the cucumbers as they disappeared one by one from Dore's plate.

Mrs. Barlow pulled some papers from her purse and put them on the table. "All we need is for one of your parents to sign this." She took a deep breath. "Look, I've never been this pushy before, but I know we can help your brother."

I licked dry lips, looking down at the crinkled papers on the table. What she said made sense.

"Why didn't you just tell my parents about the cucumbers?" I asked her.

The woman sighed. "I've tried. I called all through the school year, but no one ever answered, so I left messages. And no one called me back. I also sent home lots of letters. Did your parents ever read them?"

"I guess not." I glanced at the drawer where my parents saved their bills. It was full of envelopes with the school's address on it. And they weren't opened. I'd never even wondered why they weren't.

I picked up the papers. "Dad's in his shop," I said. "I'll find out if he'll sign them."

"I'll come with you," Mrs. Barlow said.

"No," I blurted. "You know how my dad is. I'll talk to him first."

Please sign, please sign, please sign, I said in my head as I ran to the garage. If Dad wouldn't sign, I'd make him come inside. He'd see Dore eating a cucumber. I smiled. Dad would be so excited!

I burst inside and nearly ran into my father. "Dad, Mrs. Barlow is here," I said, panting.

Scowling, Dad ran a hand over his head. "Tell her I'm not here."

"But it's about Dore." I held up the papers.

Dad grabbed them, crumpled them and tossed them in the garbage can. "You know how Daph and I feel about this," he said, scowling. "I've got to run and get some antler stain. I've got a big job to finish. I'll be back."

While Dad got into the Explorer and pulled away, I

picked the forms out of the trash. I was about as crumpled inside as those pieces of paper were. My eyes stung. The freeze-dry machine was on. It whirred and hummed softly, like it was singing along with the screechy voice of the singer on the radio who was whining about her dumb ex-boyfriend.

An idea popped into my head. I sat down at the battered desk in the corner where my dad kept his paperwork, smoothed out the wrinkled papers, and grabbed a pen.

Dore needs this, I reminded myself. *If my parents won't sign, I will.*

I'd manage things for my brother, since Mom was gone and Dad wasn't listening.

I scribbled Dad's name, fast, before I could stop myself.

After Mrs. Barlow left, Dore ate another cucumber. Then he snuggled up with his orange afghan on the sofa. Yawning, I headed to my bedroom, ready for a snooze. I pushed aside all my worried thoughts, like I was shoving them into a big box inside my head and locking it. Mom and Dad would be thrilled when they saw what Dore had learned to do at school. He could keep his clothes on, and he was eating new things. Amazing!

They'll thank me for signing those papers, I told myself.

When I opened my bedroom door, the first thing I noticed was how my white curtains fluttered in the breeze. With a squeal, I darted to the closet, but of course, Chewie's cage stood empty, because I'd left her on my bed. And I'd left the window open.

I bolted to the backyard. A breeze rustled the leaves of the apple tree in the corner. I whirled at the sound, but there was no raccoon. A dog barked close by and I wrapped my arms around my middle to keep from shaking. What if a dog already got her?

Swallowing hard, I kept up my search, calling softly for my fuzzy friend. There was no sign of Chewie in the juniper trees behind our back fence. I checked the garbage can, the woodpile, and the pink plastic playhouse bleached almost white by the sun. Still nothing. I sank down on the back steps and squeezed my eyes closed. A few tears rolled down my cheeks.

Finally, I went inside and called the only person who would understand.

"Oh, no, Lizza," Brooklyn said when she answered. "That's awful! But I bet she'll be back. Leave some grapes outside for her."

"I can't! If she comes back when Dad is around, he'll call animal control."

"Sorry," Brooklyn whispered.

When I hung up, I blew my nose and sat in the kitchen, picking at my chewed-up fingernails. What was I going to do? Would I ever see Chewie again?

The phone rang, so I answered, sniffling.

"Crapo Taxidermy?" a woman's voice said.

Sigh.

"Yeah?"

"Is my squirrel done, yet?" the lady said.

"Your...uh, your what?" I said.

"My *squir-rel*," she answered, saying the word slowly, like I couldn't speak English and was super stupid on top of that. "Mr. Crapo said it would be ready by now."

"Uh, I guess," I said, even though I had no idea. I wasn't in the mood to be helpful.

"Good. I'll be by soon to pick it up."

I put the phone down. Some crazy woman wanted a *stuffed squirrel* in her house? Even though my heart hurt, curiosity got the better of me and grabbed me by the ear to pull me outside. As much as I hated Dad's "workshop of death," I could handle sticking my head inside the place for a quick look at that squirrel.

When I opened the shop door, a strong whiff of paint stung my eyes. The lights of the freeze-dry machine blinked on and off. They'd never done that before. I turned on the light switch and yelped.

Dad had left a can of red paint on a high shelf. It had fallen onto his work table and exploded. I froze in horror, blinking a thousand times in disbelief.

Splatters of bright red paint dripped from every single dead animal on the table, including the lady's squirrel. The little guy wore a tiny cowboy hat and held a mini six-shooter in one paw and a doll-sized stack of playing cards in the other. It was too much for me. I started laughing, or maybe crying. I couldn't tell which.

Then I looked down. Tiny red paw prints dotted the floor. My raccoon had left screaming red evidence of her crime all over Dad's shop.

"Chewie?" I called.

Something rustled in the corner by Dad's old Honda motorcycle that didn't run. I tiptoed toward it and Chewie poked her head out from behind a deflated tire. With a sob, I picked her up and brought her back inside. Once in my room, I tucked her inside her carrier, where she settled down and munched on carrots. Wiping away happy tears, I hurried outside again.

First, I took Rosie's paint-splattered cage and put it outside on the grass in the back yard. I'd have to clean the cage later. Then, I ran back to the shop. I wasn't sure what to do about the garage floor, but I had to try *something*. The hose we kept coiled at the side of the house was extra-long, so I dragged it through the little side door. Dad had put a special nozzle on it that made the water spray out at supersonic speed. Plus, the water was always hot when it first came out since the hose sat under the burning Moab sun. I figured the heat might help wash the paint away from the cement floor.

It didn't.

Even worse, I lost control of the hose as I tried to spray off a dead elk's head. Water spurted all over, knocking Dad's tools to the floor and adding to the mess. Now the dead animals were bloody *and* soggy.

Sparks crackled from the panel of the freeze-dry machine. I froze and stopped spraying water. The machine buzzed and made a loud pop, so I backed out of the garage, dragging the hose with me.

Okay, that hadn't gone so well. Even though I hated the sight of those poor dead animals, I'd tried to clean them off so Chewie, and I, wouldn't get into big trouble, and all I'd done was make everything worse. A gazillion times worse.

While I was coiling up the hose, the lady came for her squirrel. I showed her the garage and told her we'd had a slight problem. She refused to pay for her outlaw squirrel, since it was now wet and splattered with paint. She yelled a lot. Finally, I grabbed a deer head from the wall that had somehow missed the paint explosion. I gave it to the lady in place of her stupid ruined squirrel. She finally went away. I was glad to get her out of there, because the freeze-dry machine was still sparking and popping.

I cleaned Rosie's cage and left it in the back yard for a while so she could get some fresh air. Then I went back inside and sat with Dore, watching cartoons and waiting for Dad to come home.

I am in so *much trouble,* I kept telling myself. *Dad's going to ground me for life.*

After a few minutes of staring at the screen without really seeing anything, a whiff of smoke wafted into the room. I sniffed and wrinkled my nose at the sooty scent. If the Strickers were barbecuing for dinner, whatever they were making was definitely not going to be edible. I hugged Dore and tried not to cry.

Sirens wailed from far off. They grew louder and louder, until flashing red lights stopped right in front of my house. I bolted to my feet as someone pounded on the door. A police officer told me I needed to get out of the house in case the fire spread. I grabbed Dore and the officer led us to a place down the street where a bunch of people had gathered. Smoke poured from Dad's shop.

We stood and watched as firefighters shouted, unrolled a big hose, and squirted water onto our flaming garage. I couldn't stop shaking, thinking about what would have happened if I hadn't left Rosie's cage outside. Orange flames flowed over the walls of the garage and water hissed as it hit the fire and sent clouds of steam into the air.

What had I done? Hugging myself, I composed a haiku in my head.

> *I burned my dad's shop.*
> *Flames are shooting everywhere.*
> *Big trouble coming.*

The roof of the building collapsed, falling with a *whoosh* and a loud crash. Well, at least the proof of what Chewie had done was gone. Like the shop. A firefighter came over and asked me if I had any idea how the fire had started.

I shook my head. But when the firefighter left, I hugged Dore tightly and tears burned my eyes. I actually had a pretty good idea of what had caused the fire. Looking back, I probably should have unplugged the freeze-dry machine before I aimed the hose at it.

Mrs. Stricker was waiting for Dore and me on our front porch when we went back to our house. She sat with us in our living room, waiting for Dad to come home. The elderly woman went into the kitchen and returned with a plate of treats. She handed me a brownie. I picked at it and threw it away after a few minutes. Then we turned on the TV and stared at the moving figures on the screen. The sound was off but nobody bothered to turn it on.

When Dad pulled up, the firefighters filled him in on what had happened. He burst inside with wide eyes. His pasty face was paler than usual. Our gray-haired neighbor got to her feet and took charge, just like she had with Mom.

"I know you're relieved to find the kids safe and sound," she told him, handing him a cookie. "Hug the kids and eat something before you think about anything else. You don't want to deal with this on an empty stomach."

Dad obeyed. He squeezed us tight, then took the treat and walked into the kitchen like a zombie. The rest of us followed him. My feet dragged as I waited for my dad to say something. He was never this quiet.

"The garage is gone," he finally mumbled around a mouthful of chocolate chip cookie.

"Yes, it is." Mrs. Stricker patted his shoulder. She put a plate of microwaved tuna casserole in front of him.

"All my taxidermy orders..."

"I know," Mrs. Stricker said, pouring Dad some Kool-Aid from the fridge. "Well, you had insurance, right?"

"No. We rent this place." Dad put his head in his hands.

"Call your landlord," Mrs. Stricker said, bustling around as she stuck foil over a casserole dish and put it in the fridge. "They'll be covered. I'm sure."

Mrs. Stricker motioned for me to sit, so I did. Dore huddled under the table and wrapped his arms around my leg.

Our landlord, Ashur, answered right away. His muffled voice got louder after Dad told him the news.

"What do you mean you don't have homeowner's insurance, Ashur?" Dad blurted into the phone. "Isn't that illegal?" Dad's shoulders slumped. "Oh. Okay."

He hung up and tossed his cell phone on the table. "It isn't illegal. Ashur expects us to pay to rebuild his garage."

Dad shoved his still full plate away. For once, Mrs. Stricker didn't say anything. She got to her feet, patted my dad one more time on the shoulder, and let herself out.

I opened my mouth to tell my dad I was sorry, but then I snapped my jaw shut. I didn't know how much money it would take to build a garage, but it had to be way more than what I earned. Even if I worked at Hole N' the Rock every day for like, forever.

"I'm gonna see if there's anything I can save," Dad said in a tired voice. When he got up, Dore and I followed him out to the yard. Hazy smoke filled the air. The stinking pile of burned rubble that used to be our garage still smoldered. Blackened wood stuck up in places like jagged, broken teeth. A couple of firefighters walked over to talk to Dad. One of them shoved a bit of wood aside with his foot and pointed at something.

With Dore holding tight to my hand, I edged closer. A few red paw prints dotted the cement at our feet.

"Raccoon prints," a firefighter said. "I bet it chewed on some wires." He took off his helmet and scratched his sweaty dark head.

Dad looked sharply at me, but then turned his back as another firefighter pointed out some frayed wires they'd fished from the rubble. Another guy picked up a crispy deer head, holding it by its antlers.

"Too bad these trophies are all ruined," he said.

I held a hand to my mouth and almost gagged. I bolted back to the house to call Brooklyn. Dore came along and curled up next to me on the booger-green couch while I dialed my friend's number.

When she answered, I blubbered the whole story.

"Oh, no," she said. "We saw the smoke. I can't believe that was your garage!" Then, she gasped. "Rosie?"

"She's okay," I said. "She was in the back yard."

"I'm so glad," Brooklyn said. "Are *you* ok?"

"No," I wailed. "Chewie got in there and chewed up the wires on Dad's machine. She caused the fire." I swallowed hard. Chewie caused the fire because I'd been irresponsible, leaving her out of her cage with the window open. I wasn't being completely honest. Why was I still lying to my best friend?

"Oh, my heck! Was Chewie hurt in the fire?" Brooklyn asked.

"No," I said with a sniff. "She's safe and back in her carrier."

"Thank goodness."

Dad walked in, and I held my breath. How much had he heard? But he just waved tiredly at Dore and me, and my little brother got up and ran to him. Dad picked him up.

"I'm going to bed," he mumbled, and the two disappeared down the hall.

And then Brooklyn said something that gave me a lump in my throat.

"Listen, okay?" she said, stopping to take a deep breath. "I hate to say this right now, but you've got to find another home for Chewie. You can't keep her hidden from your dad forever, and after today, well…"

"I know," I said in a tiny voice.

"Can you call the guy from the Humane Society? I'll help you get her to him."

"It's too far away," I said.

"Oh, come on, Lizza," Brooklyn said, her voice unusually impatient. "You have to get that poor raccoon out of the house, and fast. It's not really fair for her to be stuck in a cage all the time, is it?"

I picked at some lint on my capris. She was right, dang it!

"Okay," I said with a sigh. "But I don't want her to leave town. Do you know anybody who'd want a pet raccoon?"

"Is there anyone at Hole N' the Rock who'd take her?" Brooklyn asked. My mood lifted a tiny bit as Zochee's face came to mind. Maybe she'd like a pet.

I told Brooklyn I'd call her later and dialed Zochee's number. She answered on the first ring and laughed when I asked her if she wanted a pet raccoon. But when she understood I was serious, she told me to call Doug.

"He loves strays. He already has a cat and a…"

"So, he just might take a raccoon!" I interrupted.

Zochee laughed. "Only one way to find out."

I called Doug. He got all excited when I told him about Chewie. "Sure, I'd love to take her!"

Tears pricked my eyes. "Could I visit her sometimes?"

"You bet."

I gave him Brooklyn's address and he said he'd meet me there. Tiptoeing down the hall, I did my best to ignore the heaviness in my chest. It was obvious I had to give Chewie away. I didn't have a lot of other options. Or *any* other options.

I knocked softly on Dad's door, but he didn't answer, so I stuck my head in the room. He was out cold, with Dore curled up at his side. The lines around his eyes and mouth were carved a lot deeper than I remembered. How did he suddenly get so old-looking? It threw my world off-balance, like there was a stranger in front of me.

Dad held Mom's photo in his hand. The image of her face smiling at me made my eyes sting.

Tapping Dad's arm, I opened my mouth to tell him what really happened to the garage. But he snorted and rolled over, and I lost my nerve. Nothing could be done about the garage, now. Knowing what I'd done would only make Dad madder than ever.

I eased Dad's door closed and hurried to get Chewie out of the house. I stuck the carrier onto my bike basket and bounced over our bumpy lawn. Blinking away tears, I zoomed away toward Brooklyn's house.

My friend stroked Chewie's soft head as she waited with me. The little brown and black raccoon closed her eyes. I pretended my heart wasn't being cut in two with a dull butter knife at the thought of losing her.

We waited for Doug at the corner, since Brooklyn's parents would probably wonder what we were doing. Doug drove up in a Volkswagen straight out of a junkyard. It was orange in a few places and rust everywhere else. When he got out of his car, sunlight made his bald head shiny.

"I promise to take good care of her," he told me.

Swallowing hard, I handed him the carrier. He put it inside his VW and got back into the driver's seat.

And then, he was gone.

Brooklyn snuck me into her room through her window. Her mom knew I was still grounded and I didn't want to get caught, but I totally needed a place to cry without somebody asking me what was wrong. My bestie understood. She let me sit on her fluffy bed and blubber as long as I needed to. When I stopped, she brought me one of her mom's green smoothies, the kind I liked with lots of pineapple in it. I told my friend how Chewie ended up in the garage and how I tried to clean up her mess. And then I told her about the chewed wires.

"So, I guess it was all my fault." I put my empty glass down.

"Oh no, Lizza," Brooklyn said, her green eyes wide.

"I know," I whispered. I picked pineapple out of my teeth. "I didn't mean for anything to happen, Brooksie, honest. I was only trying to fix things."

"I'm sure your dad will understand." Brooklyn sat next to me and squeezed my arm.

"I don't think he will." I shook my head. "That's why I didn't tell him what happened."

"I get it, but if you don't tell him the truth, that's not honest, is it?" Her eyebrows met in the middle. I always hated it when they did that. "Just tell your dad about the raccoon," she added. "He *will* be mad at first, but he's your dad. He loves you."

"I can't." I jumped up. My eyes stung. "I wasn't supposed to rescue any more animals this summer, especially not any raccoons. Please, Brooks! You've got to understand!"

"I do," Brooklyn said. "But right now, I wish I'd never helped you mess up your dad's sign. Things are getting crazy. I think what we did is what's causing all this bad stuff to happen."

"No way! That's not true." I shook my head so my hair whipped around my face. It still smelled like smoke. "This isn't anyone's fault. Stuff just happens."

Brooklyn frowned up at me without answering.

"Please swear you won't say anything about this," I asked her. "I know things will work out okay if you don't tell on me. Promise?"

"Of course I won't." Brooklyn crinkled her forehead with worry, but she gave me a quick hug. "It's up to you to tell. It won't come from me."

"Thanks," I said, hugging her back. "I knew I could count on you." I waved and headed for her bedroom window.

She waved back and gave me a tiny smile.

When I got home, Dore was watching cartoons in the front room and Dad was still asleep. My brother and I shared dinner. Cheetos, bananas, and watermelon. I ate the same thing but without the ketchup.

While we were finishing, Dad came into the kitchen and tossed an empty green suitcase onto the scarred linoleum. "Time to pack. You get Dore's stuff, okay, Lizza?"

"What? Why?" I asked. "What do you mean, Dad?" I jumped up from my chair.

Dad turned around. His eyes were puffy and he scowled. "Ashur doesn't have homeowner's insurance. *I* don't have renter's insurance. We'll have to pay for all the damage." My dad jammed his hands into his pockets and shook his head. "I just took out a loan to buy Hole N' the Rock. I paid for a new billboard with my credit card, and all my taxidermy orders and my equipment just turned into a stinking pile of ashes. We're not just broke, Liz. We're in debt up to our eyeballs. We owe way more than we have. I can't pay rent anymore. We're moving."

A spike of pure terror shot through me. "But where will we go?" I whispered.

Dad rubbed his hand over his scalp. "There are fourteen rooms in the cave-house. There's room for us."

A piece of watermelon stuck in my throat. "No, Dad!" I said. "You can't be serious!"

Dad put his fingers to his temples like he does when his head hurts. "We're broke, Lizza," he said. "But there's a place where we can live rent free. Do the math!" He turned and stalked out of the kitchen.

I burst into tears. I tried not to, but I couldn't stop the waterworks. We were leaving our home, and it was my fault. Dore patted me on the leg.

Sobbing, I called Brooklyn and asked for an emergency sleepover. When I told her why, she cried, too.

And in about five minutes, Heidi's white SUV pulled up outside. She came in, talked to Dad, and had me grab some things for myself and Dore. She even let me get Rosie's cage. Then my brother and I got into the SUV and drove with her to the Henderson's house.

Another haiku by me:

> *My name is Lizza.*
> *I'm moving into a cave.*
> *My life isn't fair.*

"You can't move," Brooklyn wailed, throwing her arms around me when I walked inside her house. Her permed hair tickled my nose.

"You won't be too far away, Lizza. You can still come over any time." Her mom went to the fridge and pulled out some carrot sticks. Heidi was an older version of Brooklyn, with thick blonde hair and big green eyes. She set the veggies and a tub of hummus in front of Brooklyn and me, but the sight of food made my stomach twist into knots.

"But we won't be able to ride our bikes to each other's houses anymore, Mom," Brooklyn said.

Dore hugged me tight and my throat closed. Brooklyn threw her arms around both of us.

We stood there blubbering in the middle of the Henderson's shiny kitchen, until Heidi finally shooed us down to the family room in the basement to watch a movie. She promised to make vegan brownies. She picked up Rosie's cage, crinkling her nose, and went to stick it in her garage.

"This isn't fair." I sniffled, shuffling blindly through a stack of the Henderson's Blu-rays. "My life is over!"

Brooklyn didn't say anything, because I was right. She finally grabbed a movie from the stack and handed it to me. I shrugged and put it in the player without even reading the title.

"My dad can't make us live in a cave." Saying the words out loud made my situation even more mortifying. This was, like, humiliation times infinity! I dropped onto the couch and held a flowery pillow over my face. My little brother curled up next to me and gave me a squeeze. Just then, the five-year-old twins, Corbin and Cambri, ran in. The kids waved at me, flashing their dimpled smiles.

"Hi, Dore!" Cambri shouted,

"Let's play in my room," Corbin said. Dore jumped up and let them lead him upstairs without looking back.

"Deserter," I muttered from under the pillow.

"The twins love Dore," Brooklyn said, stating the obvious. She plopped down next to me and lifted the pillow from my face. She offered me a granola bar, but I shook my head.

"I can't live in a cave," I said again.

Brooklyn hugged her knees to her chest. "But where else can you go?" she asked me softly.

"I don't know," I muttered.

We sat there in silence, watching some dumb movie about superheroes. After lots of yelling and running and three explosions, I gave up trying to watch. I curled up on the squishy pillows, about to drop off to sleep, when a sudden idea hit me. I sat up straight and grabbed my friend's arm.

"Wait, Brooks," I said, "I have an idea! Can I use your laptop?"

"Totally," Brooklyn said.

We went upstairs. Heidi had made the brownies she promised us, so Brooklyn scooped out half the pan onto a plate. The treats were so warm they didn't stay in squares but crumbled into a pile of gooey-chocolaty delicious-ness.

"Well, what's the plan?" Brooklyn asked once we were settled in her room. I turned on Brooklyn's laptop.

"I'm going to protest online," I said, talking around a mouthful of brownie.

"Huh?"

"Well, don't you remember at school how Mrs. Easton told us young people were changing bad things in their countries by posting stuff online?"

"Yeah?" Brooklyn said.

"I'll start a protest about having to live in a cave. If I get a lot of attention, maybe the protest will convince my dad to let us live somewhere else." I logged onto my favorite social media app.

"Um, Lizza, I'm not sure that's a good idea."

"Why?"

"Won't that make your parents look bad?" she asked, sitting next to me. "You don't want to make them look like they're, I don't know, like horrible parents or something, do you?" Her green eyes were serious.

My heart sank into my stomach. "I'm moving into a *cave*, Brooklyn! My dad is making me live in a hole in the ground. I'd rather live out of our car. I'd rather *eat meat*." I sniffed.

Brooklyn's eyes got huge. "Wow," she whispered. Then she brushed her wavy hair back over her shoulders and sat up taller. "Well, maybe you could at least do one of those surveys, you know? And ask people to vote: should your dad make you live in a cave, or not?"

I hugged her. "Thanks."

It only took us a few minutes to make the survey and post it. I waited for an answer. Pretty soon, I got my first vote. It was a *yes*.

Brooklyn closed her laptop. "You should give it a day, maybe," she said. "Let's check it in the morning."

"Okay," I said with a sigh.

Results of "Should My Dad Make Me Live in a Cave?" Survey:

No: 28%

Yes: 72%

Comment: I love that idea! Our society needs to get back to the simpler life.

Comment: Caves are cooler in summer and warmer in winter. Saves you money. Way to go, Dad!

Comment: Ever hear of the Flintstones? LOL

The next morning, Brooklyn and I didn't talk much while we ate cereal. The crunching sounds drove me crazy. Dore ate a banana under the table. Corbin and Cambri decided to follow him there and all three sat on the floor, giggling and tickling our feet. I couldn't even smile.

When I got up to clear off my dishes, Heidi touched my shoulder. "I'm afraid I've got more bad news, Lizza," she said. "Your dad called. He doesn't want you to bring the tarantula along. He says he doesn't want her to scare the tourists. He asked me to take it to the pet store."

My eyes stung. "But, Rosie's small," I said. "She'll fit anywhere, so I can keep her out of sight."

"She can stay here," Brooklyn said, "can't she, Mom? We'll take good care of her."

Heidi's eyes got wide. "Well, uh..."

She looked at me. Her shoulders slumped. "Yes," she said. "She can stay here. In the garage," she added. I hugged her.

Heidi put my things into her big SUV, ready to drive me to Hole N' the Rock. Dad had asked if Dore could stay with her while we cleared out our house and brought stuff to the cave, so my little brother didn't come along. And Brooklyn had to stay with him and the twins.

She hugged me tight before I climbed up into my seat.

"I'll visit you soon," she said. "Promise."

I blinked back tears as I waved goodbye. Heidi and I listened to music and didn't say much as she drove. When we arrived at my new home, she hugged me goodbye before I got out.

"Hang in there, Lizza," she said. I couldn't say anything because of the lump in my throat. The SUV pulled away and disappeared as it zoomed down the highway. I blinked back more tears.

Carrying my backpack, I went through the souvenir shop and took a deep breath before I pushed the swinging doors open. The minute I entered the kitchen, I found myself right in the middle of a tour group Zochee was leading.

"Oh, hi there," she said when she saw me. "Everyone, this is Lizza. Her family is moving in today."

My face burst into flames.

"Into *this* house?" a man with a skinny moustache asked.

"Yes," Zochee told him. "This is a real house, you know. It has electricity and plumbing." To prove it, she turned on the faucet at the sink until a thin stream of water trickled out. Zochee smiled. "Albert and Gladys lived here for many years, and now Lizza's family is going to live here, too."

All eyes turned to me. I froze.

"What made y'all decide to buy this place?" a woman asked me. She pushed round glasses farther up her nose while she squinted at me. "Was it cheap? I hear real estate is crazy expensive around here."

Zochee opened her mouth, ready to tell everyone the story of my great-grandparents, and how they'd dug this dumb house inside a rock. But I refused to stand there and listen to my most humiliating secret blabbed to a bunch of strangers.

"It was cheap," I said, "Dad got it for five bucks."

And then I pushed my way through the group and ran for the back of the cave so I could hide somewhere, anywhere, even if I had to dig out a new room with my fingernails.

But I'd made a big mistake. Why? In Great-Grandpa Albert's cave, most of the rooms were only separated by thick columns. So, even though I hurried past Zombie Donkey and into the big living room, I was still in full view of everybody. I pretended to swipe some dust off of a shelf above the fireplace and then sauntered farther into the cave. I looked back over my shoulder. The tourists were still gawking. Open floor-plan, remember?

Luckily, there were actually two rooms with doors that closed and locked. One was the big bathroom with the carved tub—the snorkeling tub. The other one was a smaller bathroom with a shower. I headed for that one. I reached for the knob and yelped as Mrs. Stricker barged out.

"Oh, Lizza," she said. She pulled me into a hug and squeezed all the air out of my lungs. The gray-haired woman smelled like breath mints and sweat. Then she held me at arm's length. "How ya holding up, sweetheart?"

"I hate this place," I said.

"I'm real sorry, sweetie," she whispered. The knot on my insides uncurled a tiny bit. Maybe Mrs. Stricker was a nosy, know-it-all neighbor, but she understood how I felt.

"Well, we're going to fetch the food from your kitchen," she said, stepping away. "The little back bedroom is yours." Then she and Dad left. With tourists still staring, I carried my stuff to my new room where stacks of boxes went all the way up to the curved ceiling. I plopped onto the bed and a puff of dust made me sneeze.

"Bless you," a tourist said.

"Thanks." I grabbed my backpack, ran for the bathroom, and shut myself in there, finally out of sight.

Sitting on the cool tiled floor, I hugged myself.

Why, why, why, why, why??? How could Dad *do* this to me?

Taking a deep breath, I tried to think. What could I do to convince Dad to move us out of here? My dumb survey sure hadn't worked. I slumped and put my chin on my hand, pulling my heavy hair back. I had no idea. Nothing. Nada. *Wala.*

My eyes filled with tears.

Mom, come back! We need you! You won't make us stay here. You'll think of something. You always do.

The tour group moved closer, and through the closed door I heard someone complain about the twenty-foot-tall white letters painted on the outside of the cave.

"They've ruined a natural wonder," a man said. I wiped a tear from my cheek with the back of my hand and smiled just a little as an idea started to form.

As soon as the tour group left, I grabbed my camera. Maybe instead of a survey, this time I'd post a video on my social media account.

First, I hit the snack machines. Why work on an empty stomach, right? After I snarfed a granola bar, I turned on my camera and hit *record.*

"This is Hole N' the Rock, a place near Moab, Utah," I said, as I walked around the parking lot. I moved the camera up to show the big white letters painted on the outside wall of my gigantic home. "People do lots of bad stuff to the environment just to make money. See what I mean? Somebody painted those letters up there. I think it looks awful. Don't you?"

With a tiny smile, I went back inside. Maybe I'd share

this video and then post a new survey: "Should the paint be cleaned off the rock?"

Inside, I snuck around a new tour group and went to dig out Mom's laptop from a box so I could upload the recorded video. But Dad came back just then with the Strickers, so I got stuck helping. We piled food into Gladys's old-fashioned fridge while a bunch of Japanese tourists watched. One guy took a picture while Dad plugged in our tiny microwave.

"Can't you read?" the guide said. "No photos inside the house!" She was the same guide as before, the blonde woman named Cindi who'd been mad at me for sitting in a chair.

"I'm sorry," a teenage boy said.

"Oh, it's okay." Dad shook the guy's hand. "I'm Clint. Welcome. My cave is your cave."

The boy laughed. The other tourists laughed. Dad's face split into a huge grin and he grabbed paper cups from the counter.

"Who wants a drink?" he asked, opening the fridge and pulling out a bottle of Coke.

I stared. Cindi stared. She and I looked at each other.

"Your Uncle Roger never did that," she said, looking all squinty-eyed at Dad, who now passed around a box of chocolate chip cookies.

"Hey, Cindi, could you grab some paper plates?" Dad called. "And see if you can find more cookies in any of the boxes."

"Roger never did that, either. I ain't no waitress. I'm outta here," Cindi glanced at me. "You can take over, kid." She disappeared through the swinging doors.

"But, but..." I said.

"What a great idea, Cindi!" Dad said.

And that's how I found myself leading a group of Japanese people through my great-grandparent's cave-house on the very first day I moved in. Zombie Donkey watched me sadly with his glass eyes.

I'd heard the tour enough that I had it memorized. I didn't exactly try to act all excited about the cave-house, though. I used my totally bored voice. It was the only way I could think of to protest my situation.

Even with a voice that made me sound like I was about to fall asleep standing up, I still got stuck leading more tours. After five o'clock finally came, Dad ate microwaved tomato soup while I ate some grapes and crackers and drank Dr. Pepper. Heidi brought Dore back, but Brooklyn wasn't with her. My little brother ducked under an old table covered in dusty tools, ate Cheetos and watched Sponge Bob. While Dad was busy unpacking more stuff, with his back turned, I unpacked Mom's laptop and tried to upload my video.

There was no Wi-Fi in the cave. I said a bad word, but nobody heard me because Dad was talking loudly on his phone right then.

Sniffling, I gave up for the day and headed to the cave bedroom assigned to me. First, I had to shove an old doll dressed like a shepherdess under the bed so she wouldn't look at me all night with her weird faded eyes that were almost white. I pulled back the flowery bedspread and sneezed.

Great-grandma Gladys's sheets were dusty. And scratchy.

> *Cave of my nightmares,*
> *Dolls staring with scary eyes.*
> *I want to go home.*

The next morning, I finally got to upload my new video inside the tiny office with internet. I made the new survey for it, too. And then I had to lead a bunch of tours inside my great-grandparents' dumb house because Cindi didn't come back. Brooklyn never came by, even though I was sure she would. Worn out that night, I finally checked my survey results before bed.

Survey: "Should the paint be cleaned off the rock?"
Results:
No: 68%
Yes: 32%
Comment: I've always loved the big arrow. I'd miss the turn-off without it.
Comment: Don't get rid of the painted letters. They're retro-cool. Besides, that place helps bring in the rich tourists who give us their money. Our town would shrivel up without them.

I could hardly sleep.

The national parks *bring the tourists*, I grouched to myself. *Not* this *place. Flipping fudge!* It was like the universe was against me.

The next day was Saturday. I had to lead even *more* tours, but when Doug came into the kitchen, I left my tourists standing by the big carved bathtub and ran over to him.

"How's Chewie?" I asked. "When can I see her?"

Doug grinned. "Any time. She's at my place, you know? The little blue camper back in the trees. Just don't leave the gate open."

"You live *here?*" I blurted.

"Yup."

"Nacho cheese with jalapenos," I said, forgetting that One: Brooklyn wasn't here, and Two: most people thought I was crazy when I said "words of randomness."

Doug raised one eyebrow.

"I'm just saying this is the best news I've had in a long time!" If Chewie lived out here at Hole N' the Rock, living in the cave might be bearable. Almost.

I bolted outside. Then Dad called me back. The tourists were still standing around by that bathtub. Oops. I rushed through the rest of the tour and, a few minutes later, I sat inside a little fenced-in yard, cuddling the small raccoon curled up in my lap.

I found a bit of apple on the ground and held it out to her. She ate it out of my hand as I stroked her head.

"Help me, Chewie," I whispered. "How do I get out of the cave?"

She didn't have any idea, unfortunately. I stayed with her until Dad called for me to lead another tour. And another day went by with no call or visit from Brooklyn. Where was she?

I had planned to sleep late Sunday morning. Unfortunately, tourists had other plans. The official twelve-minute tours of my cave-house ran from nine to five, every day.

Dad rushed me out of bed. Groggy and groaning, I

yawned and shuffled to the bathroom, but Dore was already inside. While I waited my turn—the other bathroom was off limits because it was part of the tour—Zochee pushed through the swinging doors, leading the first group of the day.

"Oh, hey, Lizza," she called, waving. "Good morning."

My hair hung all over my face in tangled ropes, and I wore my pink pajamas—the ones with tiny pigs all over them. I ran back to my bedroom and hid behind a screen Mrs. Stricker had given me so I'd have at least a *little* privacy. Digging out an old pair of shorts and a shirt from my backpack, I got dressed and finger-combed my hair, yanking at the worst knots. I left the cave, keeping my eyeballs glued to the floor.

I ran to the office and grabbed a Coke from the mini fridge. While I slurped my super-healthy breakfast, I called Brooklyn.

"Lizza! I miss you! How's it going?" she said.

"Totally humiliating," I answered. "I had to lead a bunch of tours. Then this morning, I was *part* of the tour. In my PJ's."

"The pink ones with pigs all over them?" Brooklyn asked.

"Yup."

"Ouch," she said. "Cringy. Have you ever thought of getting new PJ's?"

Ouch, I repeated inside my head. Maybe Brooklyn's family could afford to go out and buy whatever they wanted, but my family was "on a budget," as Dad always liked to remind us. Especially now. Frowning, I glanced down at my worn shorts and picked at a loose thread. Besides, I'd always thought Brooklyn liked my pig jammies. I changed the subject.

"Hey, you know what?" I said. "I uploaded a video and did a new survey."

"I saw it," Brooklyn said. "My parents even voted. My dad said no, but my mom said yes." She giggled.

How could she laugh? My chest tightened. Brooklyn acted like everything in my life was all sunshine, rainbows, and heart emojis. Didn't she care that I'd had to move away and live in a *cave*? I looked down at my frayed shorts again. Or, maybe my well-dressed bestie was glad her thrift-store fashionista friend was out of sight.

"I gotta go," I mumbled, even though I hadn't yet asked why she hadn't called or come by. "I just wanted to say hi."

"Lemonade," Brooklyn said, still giggling.

My mood crashed to the ground. And caught on fire.

"Pumpkin pie," I said in a soft voice. I hung up.

I sat back down and guzzled my Coke, my grouchiness like a growling bear inside my chest. I put my drink down. I had to do *something* to get my dad to move us out of here! Even if Brooklyn didn't seem to care anymore.

In between tours, I took pictures inside the cave-house. I made sure to get the bucket of rusty nails that for some reason just sat by a wall—it had been there ever since I could remember. I got a photo of dusty Zombie Donkey, with his clumsy stitches falling out and most of his fur gone. I also got a picture of all the electrical cords crisscrossing the cave floor. And I finally took a photo of the gross clogged toilet that stayed unusable for a whole day, since Dad was too busy to take care of it.

At lunch time, I posted my new photos and a new survey: "Does this look like a safe place for kids?"

When I got back to the cave, Dore came up to me hugging his old Spiderman toy tightly to his chest. He'd dug it out of a box and now wouldn't let go of it.

"Hey." I held out my arms and he folded himself into my hug. "Spiderman's your new friend, huh?" While Dore snuggled into me, Spiderman's sharp, plastic fingers poked my gut. Mom was *not* going to be happy about this doll. It had taken us a year to get it away from Dore in the first place.

"Come on," I said. "Let's go see Chewie."

We went out into the parking lot. The thousand-degree weather made it hard to breathe. Blinking and squinting against the glare, we walked through the sagebrush and sand behind the parking lot to Doug's little square camper.

Dore's face lit up when he saw the raccoon. We went inside the wire fence and closed the gate behind us. Chewie came right up to me, and I gently picked her up and put her in Dore's lap. He stroked her soft fur and my heart did a happy dance. Dore loved Chewie as much as I did! We beamed at each other as we petted the cute raccoon.

My brother would probably have been content to sit there forever. I could have stayed there forever and a day, but the desert heat was broiling us. We finally got up to go.

As I closed the little gate, a loud snort from somewhere nearby made me jump. Holding Dore's hand, I tiptoed toward the sound, around the corner of Doug's camper. Tied to a metal post was a small black-and-white llama. It backed away from us and snorted again. Its breath smelled like rotting hay.

"Is that a llama?" I asked out loud, like a dork. Like Dore was going to answer me.

"Llama," Dore said.

I dropped to my knees, ignoring the gravelly dirt that dug into my scabbed skin, and grabbed Dore's shoulders. "Llama, Dore? You said llama? Say it again! Say llama!"

He smiled at me and hugged Spiderman, but he didn't say anything else.

We sprinted back to the office. I *had* to call mom!

We burst through the door of the little building. Dad sat in front of the computer. I forgot about everything, because Mom was on the screen and her face was wet with tears.

"Lizza?" Mom said. "And Dore! *Mahal ko kayo*, babies. I love you." Her voice shook. "I miss you guys."

I gulped. "I miss you, too, Mom. How's *Lola*?"

Mom smiled. "She's stable enough to travel, so I'm bringing her back to get treatment in the U.S."

"Yes!" A sunshine glow warmed me up inside. Dore smiled, and I bounced around like a kangaroo on caffeine.

Mom's face crumpled. "But how can I take her home when we don't even have a house to live in?"

Inside me, the sunshine feeling disappeared behind swirly, dark clouds. I stopped bouncing. Had Dad already told her what happened?

"We *have* a home, Daph," Dad said in a quiet voice. "There's plenty of room in the cave."

"The cave," Mom said. "Wonderful. First of all, I can't believe you didn't tell me right away, Clint. And how is this going to work? What about Dore and Lizza? You can't expect them—"

"It's working fine, Daphne," Dad interrupted. "Look, I didn't tell you because you have enough to worry about, so I took care of everything, babe. We have a place to live, and the kids love it."

I blinked. *The kids love it?* We loved Hole N' the Rock about as much as we'd love jumping into a pool full of slimy, dead fish.

"It won't be forever, of course," he said. "I want to build a taxidermy shop out behind the parking lot. We'll add an apartment to it. I've got an architect friend who's drawing up plans for me."

"And how much will the new shop cost?" Mom snapped. "We have student loans, Clint! How will we pay those *and* pay off the loan for that tourist trap you bought, *and* pay Ashur for burning his garage to the ground?"

Mom buried her face in her hands.

My heart got turned inside out. It was my fault the garage had burned down.

"Trust me, Daph," Dad said. But the next second, the screen went blank. Dad sat back in the swivel chair and closed his eyes. "She hung up on me," he mumbled.

Dore crawled under the desk and curled into a ball, hugging Spiderman.

I wandered back to Doug's place and sat inside Chewie's enclosure, hugging my knees to my chest and talking to the tiny raccoon while the summer wind rustled the nearby trees. It made a sound kind of like crying.

> *My mother is gone.*
> *She's a sad face on a screen.*
> *When will she come back?*

After I left Doug's trailer, I should have gone to help lead tours or stock shelves—we'd gotten in a shipment of cactus-shaped night lights and books about local ghosts. But I couldn't make myself do it. Not just yet, anyway. So instead of going inside the cave, I kept walking by the side of the big sandstone monolith that was my new home. I couldn't stop the heavy feeling dragging me down. Mom had never hung up on Dad. Ever.

Hot tears rolled down my face. Snuffling, I edged around a couple of bushes sprouting from cracks in the stone. I tripped over a root, my hands scrambling for something to break my fall.

I latched onto a blue rope dangling from somewhere above. Once I had my balance back, I craned my neck and gaped up at the side of the wall in front of me. The rock formation I lived inside was massive. It looked like a lumpy layer cake that had collapsed inside the oven of a towering giant. The wider base was topped by a taller and slightly narrower layer. And as I knew from leading the tours, it was several stories tall.

It didn't look like there was anyone up there, so I yanked hard on the rope. It was a little faded, but it still had a tight feel, like it wasn't too old or worn out. Sniffing, I glanced behind me to make sure no one was around. Of course, tons of people were around. What did I expect, I was living in a tourist trap! So, I made sure no one was watching me, kicked off my shoes, and put one foot against the rock. I put all my weight on the rope and then stuck both feet onto the wall in front of me. The rope creaked but it held me.

And maybe it was crazy, but once I made sure that rope was safe, all I wanted to do was climb. After the stupid Roosevelt incident, I kind of had to prove to myself that I still knew how to do it. Swiping the last few tears from my face, I pulled on the rope and walked up the side of my huge home.

It wasn't a hard climb at all. The rope was knotted every few feet. Soon, I was ten feet off the ground. I kept going and got to about fifteen feet up, then twenty. And thirty. The knot inside my chest loosened. I could never explain it, but whenever I climbed it was like my body got lighter and lighter the farther away I got from solid ground. Like my bones were hollow. And my mood floated skyward like a helium balloon.

I reached the spot where the rope was anchored and the surface leveled out, then I got to my feet and stood tall. I stood on a fairly flat area that formed a ledge above the house below. Even though I wasn't on the very top of the rock formation, I was still way high above the ground. If I remembered my "cave-house facts" right, I'd just climbed more than sixty feet.

"Whoa," I whispered, smiling. I had to tell the universe about my awesomeness! I opened my mouth to scream something cool, like "Zimbabwe!" or "Taco Tuesday!" but a heartbeat later I snapped my mouth shut. "Words of randomness" was my thing with Brooklyn, and she wasn't there. Besides, things were suddenly really weird between us, and I had no idea when they'd get better. Or if they ever would.

I deflated like a leaky balloon. Sighing, I sat cross-legged on top of my new home and took in the scenery.

In the parking lot below, a doll-like Zochee moved past the matchbox cars in the lot. I crouched low, so I wouldn't be as easy to spy from down there, although anyone who happened to turn their eyes toward the big rock would see me. I'd stand out against the red sandstone like a fly on a giant loaf of bread.

Something new caught my eye and I leaned forward for a closer look. Dad had stuck a big hand-painted sign in the bed of the "Mater" tow truck. It said:

FUTURE HOME OF CRAPO TAXIDERMY

Peanut butter and jelly! I grouched to myself. Dad's words about building a shop came back to me. He planned to add an apartment to it. So even if I moved out of the cave, I'd be stuck living with a bunch of dead animals.

I leaned back and blinked up into the clear blue of the sky. Even though the sun beat down on me, up here the air was cooler and filled with the smells of sagebrush and rain. I couldn't enjoy it too much, though. The sudden appearance of the sign on poor Mater down in the parking lot ruined the moment for me.

A few swallows flew by, so close I swore puffs of air from their moving wings touched my face. They soared high until they were tiny dots that dissolved into the blue.

I sighed, closed my eyes, and tried to imagine flying like that. Part of me wished I could grow wings and join them. I'd take off and never come back. I'd race through fluffy clouds, the big puffy ones that looked like cotton candy or fat sheep, and float like a kite in the wind.

And...I'd also have to eat bugs.

Ew. I sat up and came back to reality. I didn't really want to leave, I still had Dore, and that kid needed me.

"Lizza?"

I whipped my head around. Doug was up on top of my house, too. He headed in my direction, walking along the sloping red rock with a coil of rope around a shoulder, some tools in his hands, and wide eyes.

"Hey," I said.

"How did you get up here?" he asked, blinking rapidly.

"The rope," I answered. "Where did that llama come from?"

Doug laughed and sat down by me.

"She belonged to an old friend from college," he said. "He was moving and couldn't keep her, so I took her in. Her name's Priscilla. Guess you've already met."

"Yeah." I hugged my knees. "She's awesome."

"Yup." Doug smiled.

That was all either of us said for a while, but the quiet wasn't weird. Doug and I both understood we didn't have to say anything if we didn't want to. The desert below went on and on all around us, and I smiled as I took in the view of my new home from above, imagining I was a hawk or an eagle, surveying my world. Trees waved in the hot breeze and tiny people scurried around like insects swarming past the teensy toy cars.

The area behind Doug's trailer caught my eye. The wide-open space was dotted with lots of cottonwood and pine trees. A little stream sparkled as it wound through the brush. Priscilla would love it.

I sat up tall. "Hey, Doug," I said. "Do you see the big space behind your house?" I pointed.

"Yeah," Doug said. "It's nice, isn't it?"

"It's a perfect place for animals, don't you think?"

Doug opened his mouth to speak, but at that second, I happened to glance down at the tiny office on the other side of the parking lot. Dad popped out, and about the time I saw him, he looked up. He stopped short and stuck his fists on his hips. Then he raised one arm and jerked his thumb back over his shoulder in a "get your butt down here this minute" gesture.

"Uh oh," I whispered.

"Looks like you'd better go." Doug stood and headed back to wherever he'd come from.

Oh, geez. I got to my feet. Why couldn't more adults be like Doug? I sure wished my Dad would just chill once in a while.

While I climbed back to the ground, I tried to come up with an excuse to explain why I'd climbed up the rock, but I couldn't. And if I could have turned into a swallow, I just might have done it. Even if I had to chow down on bugs.

"You're grounded," Dad said when I reached him. "If tourists saw someone up there, some of them would be dumb enough to try the climb themselves. If they fell and got hurt, I'd be sued in a second."

"You're grounding me?" I said. "Why? It's not like I actually have anywhere to go. We are in the middle of nowhere." I winced. Why had I said that? I should have just stayed quiet.

Taking off the stained cowboy hat he'd started wearing, Dad swiped at the sweat on his forehead and looked around. Then, he smiled.

"You're right. No grounding. Instead, you owe me," he tilted his head as he paused, "say, two hours of chores. Clock's ticking. Go find Doug and ask him for a job." He walked off, whistling to himself.

Grrrrrr! Doug was still somewhere on top of my stone age house, so I couldn't climb back up and ask him to give me chores to do. I looked up at Roosevelt. His nostrils were still white. I'd overheard Doug say he planned to spray some reddish paint in there, since the cleaner hadn't worked. That's why he left the ladder up.

I smiled. I didn't need to ask Doug for a job, after all. I'd found one myself. And if I did this job right, it just might finally get me fired! Bonus. Still grinning, I headed to the supply closet. It was time for the old president carving to get a new, modern look. One my dad would hate.

Along with paint supplies I also found an old slinky in the closet, just like one I had when I was little. All I needed was some really strong glue, and Roosevelt would look way cooler. I left the supplies there and went in search of glue.

Inside the shop, Zochee was talking to someone on the phone. When she saw me, she turned her back.

"I'd love to," she said. "I can't wait to see you. You, too, honey." When she hung up and turned around again, her face was flushed and she was smiling.

"Need anything?" she asked me.

"That was your boyfriend, wasn't it?"

Zochee's blush deepened, but so did her smile. "Yes."

"You guys sound kind of serious," I said.

"Maybe." She unwrapped a candy and popped it in her mouth. Then she wadded up the wrapper and tossed it at me. I ducked and she smiled. "Well? Did you need something?"

"Really strong glue," I told her. "Like something that would even stick to rock?"

"Oh, Doug must have sent you for the stuff he told me to order." She reached below the counter and handed me a metal spray can. "He needed to cement an old pipe in place and said this would work."

I checked out the label. It was supposed to harden right away. Perfect.

"Okay," I said, taking the can. "Thanks."

Back in the supply closet, I swiped the slinky and searched through the spray paint cans stored in an old cardboard box on the floor. There were tons of awesome shades to choose from. The president was about to get way more interesting. I chose a great color and stuffed my supplies inside my backpack. Then I went outside to look for Dad.

I blinked in the bright sunlight and squinted around for a glimpse of him. He had to be busy doing something, or my plan would fizzle out in half a heartbeat. I jumped when he called my name from only a couple of feet away.

"I need to run into town. I'm taking Dore with me. Keep busy, okay?" he said.

I saluted. Dad shook his head and rolled his eyes. And then he was gone. Perfect.

At the foot of the ladder I glanced at the safety harness dangling above and bit my lip. The memory of my earlier rappelling "performance" made my cheeks burn but I took a deep breath. I didn't need a safety harness—I wasn't about to repeat my death-defying act. Gripping the ladder, I climbed all the way up to Roosevelt.

It didn't take long to spray over the white inside his nostrils. Then, I sprayed some of the glue Zochee had given me on one side of the rock-president's nose. It made a sticky, bubbly patch of goo. One end of the slinky stuck right into it and stayed there...so did one of my fingers. I yanked it away, ripping half my skin off with it. Grumbling to myself, I glued the other end of the slinky in place, careful not to glue my finger again.

Back on the ground, I moved away from the wall so I could get a good look at my work. I giggled and clapped my hands a couple of times. Yeah, I know, I applauded myself, but the statue was now a thing of beauty. Roosevelt had bright turquoise-colored nostrils, and the slinky made a great nose ring.

Back inside, I stuck the paint and glue back in the closet

and went to the bathroom to wash my hands. I scrubbed as hard as I could, but the super strong glue didn't budge.

Mushy peas, I grumbled to myself. I'd just have to wait until it wore off.

After grabbing my camera, I went back outside and took a bunch of pictures. I photographed Roosevelt as well as Dad's sign. Sneaking across the parking lot, moving from one statue to another, I inched closer to the office and ducked inside.

Uploading my new pictures only took a few minutes. Then I created two new surveys:

Survey # 1: "Which look do you like best for the president? The old one or the new?"

Survey # 2: "Should a taxidermy shop be built at Hole N' the Rock?"

Humming to myself, I headed back outside. A small crowd had gathered beneath the Roosevelt carving. Zochee stood there, too, with her hand over her mouth. The tourists held up phones, snapping a ton of pictures.

"That's awful," somebody said.

"I love it," somebody else said.

Zochee caught my eye. She put a hand on her hip and cocked her head to one side. Keeping my eyes innocent, I hoped, I shrugged.

Shaking her head, Zochee motioned for me to go back inside. I followed her into the shop and kept busy trying to untangle a wad of knotted necklaces.

Dad came back an hour later. He yelled really loud in the parking lot, saying words I'm not allowed to say. When I finished up with a tour group, he was waiting for me in the souvenir shop.

"What has gotten into you?" he asked, the second the last tourist trudged outside. His face burned red.

"I was just helping Doug like you told me," I said. "I gave Roosevelt a new look. I think he looks cool. Don't you?"

Dad put his hand over his eyes for a second, and I clamped my lips together to keep from smiling. He was about to fire me. Yes!

"No more helping Doug," he said through gritted teeth. "No more climbing the ladder. You stick to working in the shop, leading tours, and babysitting Dore. Go find Doug and tell him to take that ladder down." He turned his back to stomp outside. "And no allowance for a month," he shouted.

I scowled at the floor. Why wouldn't he just fire me?

Zochee told me to vacuum the bedrooms in the cave. Then I had to clean the bathrooms. Later, Doug came in, looking for his special glue. I got it from the supply closet and gave it to him, but I forgot to tell him to put the ladder away, even though Dad asked me to.

That night, I looked at my surveys online.

Results of Survey # 1: "Which look do you like best? The old one or the new?"

Old Look: 49%

New Look: 51%

Comment: This is a huge improvement. Yeah, dude!

Comment: Isn't that nose ring disrespectful?

Comment: Do you have a problem with nose rings?

Comment: Why are his nostrils blue?

Results of Survey #2: "Should a taxidermy shop be built here?"

Yes: 84%

No: 16%

I didn't bother reading the comments.

Early the next morning, Zochee came in. Her wavy hair, normally styled perfectly, was up in a messy ponytail. She wasn't wearing any makeup and her eyes were puffy and pink.

"Are you okay?" I asked her. "You look tired."

Zochee blinked at me. "I'm fine." She turned her back but not before I saw the tears in her eyes. A weight pressed into my chest.

The phone rang and Zochee answered it and handed it to me. Then she went to lead a tour.

"I love what you did with Roosevelt!" Brooklyn squealed in my ear. "That was so funny! You have the best ideas."

I smiled. This sounded more like the old Brooklyn—the one who had burping contests with me and wrote poetry about her favorite candy bars.

"I miss you, bestie. Can you please come here today?" I asked.

"Sure," she said. When I hung up, I did a happy dance. I only knocked a couple of guidebooks to the floor. And another snow globe with a scorpion inside.

While I stocked shelves, waiting for Brooklyn to come, I tried to think of something I could do to make Zochee smile. After all, she was pretty much my only friend, here. *I know, a haiku! I'm pretty good at that.* I grabbed a scrap of paper and got to work.

> *Cheer up, my new friend*
> *Things will be better real soon.*
> *You will smile again.*

I frowned. *Boring.* I tapped my pencil on the counter as I tried to come up with a better one. A few seconds later, Zochee came back through the swinging doors. She waved a tired goodbye to the tourists who tromped outside. I hid my haiku with my hand, since it wasn't ready.

Without saying anything to me, Zochee ducked behind the counter and took off her name tag. She picked up an old receipt and wrote "Xochitl" on it. Then, she taped the paper onto her name tag, covering the name "Zochee," her boyfriend's nickname for her. I grabbed my haiku and held it out to her right then, even if it was boring.

"Here," I said. "This haiku is definitely not my best one, but I didn't have a lot of time."

Zochee read it and her mouth trembled. "Oh, Lizza." She hugged me and sniffled. "Thank you, sweetie. That was so nice."

"I just wanted to make you smile," I mumbled against her shoulder. When I stood back, tears dripped from her eyes again.

"Um, so," I said, "can I go outside for a while? My friend is coming soon."

"Sure." She waved me away. "I don't have anything better to do than lead tours inside a cave." She turned her back and started picking up stuffed animals that had fallen from a display onto the floor.

Shut the front door. I went outside and slumped on a

bench. It didn't take a genius to figure out what had happened. Her boyfriend must have dumped her. What a...*banana brain!* Zochee was awesome times a million gazillion!

After grabbing some chips from the vending machine, I returned to my spot and crunched my snack, enjoying my short stretch of alone-time. Dore was with Dad, who'd driven to the nearest laundromat with a mega-load of dirty clothes. They'd probably be back soon, but for now I had a break from babysitting. When Heidi's Tundra pulled into the parking lot, Brooklyn jumped out and ran over. I was still on the bench, watching German tourists take pictures of some of the French tourists who were yelling at Italian tourists about a soccer game. My friend bounded over to me with a big smile and pulled out a mega-sized jar of almond butter from her bag.

"Happy Friday!"

I jumped up and threw my arms around her. "Let's eat!" Even though I hurt for Zochee, my world suddenly got a lot brighter. The girl in front of me with the wavy yellow hair and green eyes sure looked and acted like the old Brooklyn.

We hid inside my cave bedroom while tourists walked by on the other side of the lacy screen. My friend and I sat on the dusty bed and ate almond butter with celery stalks. Then we drank orange sodas and had a burping contest until Zochee chased us outside. While we walked down the paths of the cactus garden, I told Brooklyn about Zochee's breakup, and she helped me come up with a new haiku.

> *How could you dump me?*
> *Maybe I was just too good.*
> *You big, mean poop head.*

It was terrible, but we laughed at it anyway. We actually laughed so hard people stared at us. We ducked into the trees behind the parking lot to hide from all the eyes pinning us down and sat on a flat area of ground. When we finally stopped giggling, it got so quiet I could hear squirrels scrambling in the branches above our heads and suddenly, nothing was funny anymore. I still didn't know why Brooklyn hadn't once stopped by for a visit.

"Hey, Brooks," I said, finally working up the nerve to ask her, "what's going on? Why haven't you at least called me before now? I've been stuck out here for a whole week."

Brooklyn's face turned pink. "I'm sorry," she said. "I've been busy with stuff. And, well, it's hard when I can't just take my bike over to your house any time I want to."

So, you just forgot about me? I wanted to say, but I bit my lips to keep from blurting it out.

"How's Rosie?" I asked after a second.

"Great," Brooklyn said. "The twins love her. My mom's even getting less afraid of her."

"Good."

We walked in the trees for a while, listening to the low sound of voices from the parking lot. Usually, we couldn't stop talking when we were together. Today, I didn't know what else to say to my own best friend. I cleared my throat.

"My social media posts aren't working," I said. "Everybody thinks the cave is great." I kicked at a pebble in my way. "This morning Dad even told me the newspaper called and wanted to take pictures of Roosevelt. He's leaving the nose ring up there until they do. He thinks a story in the paper will get more tourists."

"It's like everything you do gets *more* people to want to visit," Brooklyn said. "It doesn't help you move out. What else do you think you can do?"

I sighed. "I have no idea. Zip. Zero, Zilch. Nothing. Nada. *Wala.*"

Brooklyn giggled. "Well, at least you tried. Right?"

"Yeah." I yelped as Dore knocked into me. I hadn't even heard him walk up to us. Giggling, he wrapped his arms around me and squeezed, and then he hugged Brooklyn.

"I've missed you, Dore," she said, tickling him. Dore squealed with laughter.

"Hey, have you seen your dad's new billboard?" Brooklyn asked me.

I stared. "His what?"

"Uh oh, I thought you knew," Brooklyn said. "Here, I took a photo." She handed me her phone.

The picture gave me the funny feeling you get when you don't know what to do with your hands. Or the feeling you get when you wish you were on another planet. In another universe.

I groaned. "Oh, *zebra spit*! This is so much worse than the last one!"

"I know," Brooklyn said softly.

The new billboard was a giant photo of the country star, Clint Brown, the one my dad loved. He held a deer head in one arm and made a "thumbs up" sign with his other hand.

I've never seen a dead animal look this alive, the sign read above his head. My dad must have photoshopped it. There wasn't any other way to explain that *bleeping* sign!

"Why does my family have to be so embarrassing?" I groaned. I handed the phone back to Brooklyn.

"I didn't know your dad knew Clint Brown," she said, looking down at the picture. "That's kind of cool, isn't it?"

"He *doesn't* know him," I said. "I can't believe he used his picture. Let's go back inside. I need some sugar."

But before we got too far, a bus pulled into the parking

lot and stopped with a loud screech of brakes. Dore jumped, squealed, and bolted away from us.

"Stop!" I shouted, but my brother didn't listen. He swerved between cars in the parking lot, his curly head bobbing in and out of sight before disappearing completely.

"Oh, no," I groaned. "Dad's going to kill me."

"Come on," Brooklyn said. "I'll help you find him."

We darted into the lot, which suddenly got a lot more crowded as people climbed down from the tour bus. I dodged a bunch of old ladies wearing sun hats and carrying big purses. I screeched around a man pushing a walker. He scowled and shouted, "Watch where you're going, missy!"

Dore was nowhere in sight. Brooklyn and I ran into the souvenir shop and darted into each room of the cave-house. We even checked the big bathtub, but Dore wasn't tucked inside, hugging his Spiderman doll.

Brakes squealed outside and someone screamed. I stopped breathing and my heart turned to ice. I turned to Brooklyn, her eyes popped wide like mine, our mouths open like a couple of fish gasping for water.

We ran outside, while inside my head I screamed *no, no, no!*

A big brown car idled inches away from Dore. He stood frozen, staring at the front bumper like a mouse caught in the sights of a giant cat. Brooklyn squealed, but my throat tightened around a scream that stayed stuck inside.

The driver burst out of the car, darted over to my brother, and knelt down, wrapping her arms around him. Tears streamed down Mrs. Barlow's face.

"Oh, Dore!" she wailed. She hugged him even tighter while she turned her wet face toward me and Brooklyn.

"Where are your parents? I nearly killed this sweet boy!"

Dad ran over to us and Mrs. Barlow stood, still clutching Dore's hand. "I'm so sorry," she sobbed over and over.

"It wasn't your fault." His voice shook. He picked up my whimpering brother and Dore buried his head in Dad's neck. Mrs. Barlow finally calmed down enough to get back in her car.

"I'm never going to drive fast again," she said tearfully. She backed up the brown Honda and eased it out of the parking lot and onto the highway, where she drove off at a crawl.

"I forgot to ask her why she was here," Dad said as we watched her disappear around a curve.

The lump in my throat wouldn't let me talk. I wouldn't have said anything, anyway. Now was not the time for Dad to learn about those papers I'd signed.

My teeth chattered and my breath came out in short gasps. Brooklyn called her mom and we waited on a bench outside the souvenir shop. Without even mentioning the cost, Dad handed me and my friend candy bars and a bag of Cheetos for Dore.

Heidi made it in record time. When her SUV pulled up, Dad told me to ask her if Dore and I could both go home with Brooklyn. Of course, Heidi said yes.

And even though my heart still galloped around inside

my rib cage like a herd of stampeding horses, hope filled my whole body. Was my dad saying what I thought he was saying?

"You mean we don't have to live here anymore?" I asked.

Brooklyn squealed and threw her arms around me. But Dad's next words shredded the sudden feeling of happiness that had just started to glow inside.

"No." He ran his hands through his thinning hair. "I meant just for tonight."

He crossed the parking lot and headed for the office. My eyes stung. I whirled around and ran to my bedroom to grab a few things, blinking and sniffling.

We could have lost Dore. This place really wasn't safe, with a big parking lot always jammed with cars, jeeps, and SUVs, just a few steps away from our home. Why wouldn't my dad understand we couldn't stay?

When Dore, Brooklyn, and I got to the Henderson's house, my little brother ate cucumbers and bananas and sat down to watch videos with the twins. My friend and I grabbed snacks and went to get Rosie. I let her roam around for a while as we sat in Brooklyn's room.

"Why can't I just live *here*?" I flopped onto the window seat.

"I wish you could," Brooklyn said with a tiny smile. She offered me a Ding Dong, and I took it. Eggs were in the ingredients, but I had a rule to never say no when offered a Ding Dong. That would just be rude.

Sitting cross-legged, I leaned back against the wall and licked chocolate off my thumb. "I was so sure Dad was going to...never mind." Disappointment stabbed me so hard my chest actually hurt.

"I know," Brooklyn whispered.

We ate, licking chocolate off our fingers and listening to the breeze rustle the leaves of the trees outside.

Brooklyn's phone beeped. "Hey, your dad forwarded a text." She held the screen up for me. She picked up Rosie and cradled her in her hand while I read the text.

Mama and I are heading home. Will get to Salt Lake late Sunday night. It was from Mom. Hope barreled back, shooting all through me.

"Yes," I shrieked, getting to my feet to dance. "Mom's coming back, and she's bringing my *lola* with her! I can't wait to see her! And you know what's the best part?"

"What?" Brooklyn said, laughing as she put Rosie back in her cage.

"Mom will fix this!" I said. "She'll know what to do." I was positive she would. Mom always had the answer for anything.

Suddenly, Brooklyn and I were talking like we used to. We laughed and joked. There wasn't this uneasy silence like before. It was the magic of my mom coming back. She made everything better.

Heidi yelled up the stairs for Brooklyn, wondering where Rosie's cage was. With guilty faces, we brought her downstairs and put the tarantula back in the garage.

"Thank you," Heidi said with a tiny shiver when we came back to the kitchen. She picked up a box from the counter.

"Here are a couple of your old dolls, back and good as new, Lizza," she said. "These were the only ones not smashed to smithereens."

"Are these some of Gladys's creepy dolls? Why were they sent to *you?*" I took the box from her.

"My cousin Mira repairs antique toys," Heidi said with a grin. "I got your dad a good deal."

"Wow, thanks," I said. We went to Brooklyn's bedroom. I pulled out the first doll and my friend shrieked and jumped onto her bed.

"What?" I turned the toy over in my hands. "Oh, eesh!" My lips pulled down at the corners and I wrinkled my nose.

The creepy doll looked like a twelve-inch tall vampire in a dusty dress the color of moldy oatmeal. Tiny cracks covered her pale face, and yellowish smears of glue leaked out from the break lines. One of the doll's painted eyes was higher than the other. The worst part was how the doll's blood-red lips parted in a wide smile and showed off a row of tiny, pointed teeth.

"Maybe she's possessed." I held the doll out toward Brooklyn. She screamed and covered her face with her hands, and I gave the doll a squeaky voice.

"Brookieeeeee..." I wailed, "I want to be your friend! Give me a hug!"

"Stop it!" Brooklyn screamed, but she laughed, too.

After we finally stopped giggling, we shoved the vampire doll under a pillow and pulled the other doll from inside the box. It was creepy, too, but in a different way. It was a clown with yellow dots all over its clothes and tangled orange curly hair glued onto its head. Its face was stuck in a "yes, I *am* crazy" grin. Its arms reached forward, like it wanted to grab someone.

"This one is just as scary." I tossed the clown back into the box.

"I know," Brooklyn said, giggling. She shuffled through her dresser drawer until she found her inhaler and puffed it into her mouth. "We *have* to make a video about these dolls. Remember how we used to do that?" she wheezed out.

"That's an awesome idea." Brooklyn and I used to make

stop motion videos with our old dolls. It was a lot of work but always fun.

After I got Dore settled in a sleeping bag in the twins' room, Brooklyn and I worked on our new project. We made a stop-motion video, using pictures of the cave-house as a background for the action. I wrote the script. It was amazing.

We worked late. We kept going with stolen Pepsis and more hard-to-resist Ding Dongs.

By 2:30 a.m., I was hoarse from recording scary doll voices, and Brooklyn couldn't keep her eyes open. I set our video to upload to my social media site—I had to share this amazing art with the world.

We called our video, "Cave of the Demon Doll." Demented Dora, the vampire doll, moved around in jerky stop motion, casting spells and cursing everybody. We borrowed my sleeping brother's Spiderman doll for the video, and poor Spidey was forced to sing and dance the Macarena for a thousand years as a punishment for insulting Demented Dora. The clown doll got on Dora's bad side, too, so he got turned into that annoying pop star kid, Trystin Beemer, whose songs made me want to tear my ears off my head.

"You know," Brooklyn said, yawning the words out, "that was way fun."

"Yup," I yawned back, scrunching down into my sleeping bag.

"Good night," Brooklyn said. "Creepy clowns."

I giggled. "Vampire teeth," I answered. Words of randomness. I smiled as I drifted off to sleep. I had the old Brooklyn back. And Mom was on her way home with *Lola*!

When I awoke, I sat up and yawned, grimacing at the

death-breath taste in my mouth. Brooklyn sat cross-legged on her bed with her laptop in front of her.

"Oh, my heck," she said, glancing at me with wide eyes.

"What?" I asked, scratching my head.

Brooklyn turned the laptop screen in my direction.

"*Sugar cookies*," I said. "Cave of the Demon Dolls went viral!"

We ate Frosted Flakes with chocolate almond milk while we read some of the comments.

MissCrazyCat2559: This is wicked! Want to do a collaboration video with me? Your work is brilliant!
Serenity Spirit Seekers: Are you sure the porcelain doll isn't truly possessed? We've seen cases like this before. Contact us and we can examine her.
RastaDude09: Whut da freak did I watch? Now I'll have nightmares!

When we got back to Hole N' the Rock around 10:30 that morning, a woman stood by the parking lot entrance, holding up a big sign.

"Hey!" I said. "What's that lady doing?"

"What?" Brooklyn and her mom said at the same time. Dore giggled.

The woman, a pretty twenty-something-year-old with red hair and sunburned skin held a sign that said: "Keep Natural Wonders Natural." She wore a white summer dress and had a circle of flowers in her hair.

"Hmph," Heidi said with a snort. "Looks like she's trying to protest something about this place. Don't worry about it, Lizza."

Brooklyn and I looked at each other. "Do you think she saw what you posted online?" my friend whispered.

Nodding, I hugged myself. Dad didn't like people who did this kind of thing. In fact, he got all cranky over stuff like this. He said protestors were just losers who had nothing better to do than try to cause trouble.

Dad waved from his office. He came out to get Dore and told me to go work in the shop. He narrowed his eyes every time he glanced over at the lady with the sign.

I waved to Brooklyn as Heidi drove away. Then, I carried the demon dolls inside. Zochee wrinkled her nose when she saw them. Smiling, I put them back in Gladys's bedroom. I stuck Demented Dora on top of a pillow, and then I made the other dolls cover their eyes or hide their heads under crocheted blankets. Zochee rolled her eyes but didn't say anything to me.

I stuck Crazy Clown inside the green leaves growing from the planter in the kitchen. It looked like he was leaning forward, ready to jump out. It was genius. Humming to myself, I went to stock shelves in the shop. About five minutes later a loud shriek came from the kitchen. I couldn't help it, I giggled.

"Get that doll out of there, Lizza," Zochee told me. "It's scaring people." Her eyes were still puffy and red.

"Hey, are you okay?" I asked after I stuck the clown on a bedroom shelf.

Zochee sniffed. "No. But thanks. I'll be fine." And after giving my arm a quick squeeze, she went to lead another tour.

At lunchtime, I met Dad and Dore inside the tiny maintenance shed where Doug kept his equipment. We squeezed into the one-room building and sat at a folding table to eat most of our meals. Even Dad was tired of eating in the cave-house while tourists walked past, staring.

"I can't wait to see Mom," I said, bouncing on my squeaky folding chair. "She'll be back later tonight, right?"

Dad kept his eyes on his plate. "Yeah," he mumbled.

"Yes!" I shouted. Dore grabbed my arm and squeezed, his brown eyes gleaming.

Dad took a long swig of his root beer. "I'm leaving for Salt Lake so I can pick up Mom and your grandma from the airport."

"Can we stay up until you guys get back?" I asked.

Turning to look at me, Dad's face went blank. He blinked a few times and stood up. He opened the door and stood there for a second, looking outside. Finally, he answered. "No, I'm taking your mom and Marita directly to the Strickers' house when we get back. In fact," he said, finally turning around to look at me, "that's where they'll be staying for a while."

I'd figured that might happen, because there wasn't any more room in the cave. We had plenty of bedrooms, yeah, but they were all part of the tour. When Dad said "for a while" he had to actually mean, "until we find a new home." I was sure of it.

Stopping to take a deep breath, I watched Dad's tired eyes. Why did my heart suddenly speed up like I was running? I took a quick drink of my soda before I got enough courage to speak. "I know there isn't room for them to stay here," I said. "So, when are we moving back to Moab?" There! I'd said it.

Dad shook his head. He rubbed his hand over his eyes. "Lizza, we're not moving back to Moab. This is our home, now," he said in a tired voice.

Dore grabbed my arm again. His eyes gleamed with tears and his chin trembled.

"But what about what happened to Dore yesterday, Dad? The parking lot isn't safe. He could have been..." I gulped. I couldn't say the word, so I moved on. "What about the protestor?" I asked. "Didn't you see her?"

Dad rolled his eyes. "Oh, yeah. About that. Have Zochee text me if any more nut-jobs show up when I'm gone. I'll call the cops."

"Dad—"

"I have to get going, Lizza. Keep your eyes on your brother at all times. We can't have any more near misses like yesterday. I need you to be more careful." He left, letting the door bang shut behind him.

My little brother dove into my lap and wrapped himself around me. I hugged him tight, and we sat there for a long time. Voices babbled outside as tourists stopped for ice cream, cheap souvenirs, and tours of my ugly home. Our old Explorer whined as Dad headed out of the parking lot. He was picking up my mom. But she wouldn't be staying with us. With her family. I thought up a haiku.

> *My mother is gone*
> *She will not come back to me*
> *What did I do wrong?*

After a while, Dore got up and pulled on my arm. I let him lead me to my cave bedroom where most of our stuff was still in boxes. He grabbed his Spiderman doll and the portable DVD player and curled up on the bed. I sat beside him and kissed the top of his curly head. He didn't look up from the flickering screen in his hands. With a sigh, I headed to the souvenir shop and asked Zochee if she'd keep an eye on my brother.

She nodded, so I went back outside for a walk. The red-headed lady was still there, and so were three more people, with three new signs.

Protect Mother Earth.
Love All Creatures, Don't Eat Them.
Clean Off This Rock!

Wow. I bit my lip and stuffed my hands into my pockets. It sure looked like these guys *had* found the stuff I'd posted online.

"What should we do, Lizza?" Zochee said, hurrying up from behind. She watched the protestors with her hands on her hips. "Do you think I should tell your Dad? I hate to bother him when he's so worried about so many things." She frowned as one of the protestors, a skinny guy with dreadlocks, turned and waved at us with a big smile.

I flushed and twiddled my fingers at him in a return wave, making sure Zochee didn't see me.

"Let's wait for a while," I told her. "I don't want to make Dad worry. I'm sure they'll go away soon."

"Do you really think so?" Zochee looked down at me with a crinkled forehead.

I took a deep breath. "Yes. Don't call my dad yet."

"If you say so." She turned back to the souvenir shop.

Kicking at a pebble, I watched her leave. It didn't look like the protestors would just go away. I didn't *want* them to go away. I ducked inside the shop to grab water bottles and then sprinted back outside.

"Here," I said, handing around the bottles.

The four protestors smiled and thanked me.

"That's so nice," the red-headed one said.

"What made you decide to come here?" I asked her.

"My friend shared a funny video online and it led me to some other posts and videos about this place. They were about the defacement of a natural formation in the desert and a taxidermy shop coming in."

"Oh," I said. "Wow." I *was* the reason these guys were here. *Snickerdoodles!*

"Are more people coming to protest?" I asked her.

She smiled. "We're just getting started."

I smiled back. And then I brought them microwave burritos.

Dad got back to the cave about three in the morning.

"Mom?" I whispered. "And *Lola?*"

"They're fine," Dad whispered back. "Is your brother in there with you?"

"Yeah."

"Good. Go back to sleep."

Dore sighed and shifted but didn't wake up. He'd fallen asleep at the foot of my bed, curled up around his Spiderman doll. I'd just left him there since Dad had gone and the sweet kid would have had to sleep all alone in the living room, his usual nighttime spot. I tucked Dore's favorite afghan around him and flopped back onto my pillow.

A few hours later my alarm went off, yanking me out of a wonderful dream. In my dream, I was watching TV in our old house while I held Chewie on my lap, and Rosie wandered around the living room, free. The old dog Gary was there, too, drooling all over my feet. And even Mom was there. Her off-key singing floated to my ears from somewhere in the house. Forced awake by my screeching alarm, I groaned and pulled covers over my head.

Why did I have to wake up just now? I shook my head. The cave-house smelled like dust and cool stone, and the smell was in everything—even the blankets on my bed. I muffled a sneeze.

"You guys up?" Dad mumbled from his sleeping spot in the living room. He yawned. "Guess we should get going, huh? Your mom can't wait to see you guys."

My foggy brain finally woke up all the way. Mom was home! Throwing the covers off, I sat up and jiggled my little brother. He was still out cold at the foot of the bed, wrapped in Grandma Thora's orange afghan and hugging Spiderman. I smiled. He'd been sleeping better lately and didn't take his clothes off half as often. I couldn't help thinking it was because I'd cut all the tags out of his clothes.

"Dore," I whispered, "Mom and *Lola* are home." I stroked his soft face. "We get to see them today."

Dore sat up, smiled, and held his arms out to me. I pulled him onto my lap and hugged him, burying my face in his soft, dark curls, breathing in his sweet smell.

"Mom," he whispered.

"Dore, you are *talking*, buddy!" I said. He laughed, and we tickled each other for a while. I helped Dore get dressed while Dad showered.

We finally headed to town. Dad didn't say much, except to ask me if I'd combed my hair, (no), and why my socks didn't match. (Because I liked them that way).

"Coconuts!" I shouted when we got to Moab.

"What about coconuts?" Dad asked.

"Nothing," I said. "I felt like saying it, so I did. Coconuts, coconuts, COCONUTS!" I shouted. What a perfect word. It could stand for anything, good, bad, or ugly. Today it stood for the awesomeness of *Mom is back and Lola is here!*

When we got to our old neighborhood, Mom was waiting for us on the Strickers' porch, sitting cross-legged on the steps. She leapt to her feet and sprinted across the yard the minute our Explorer turned onto our old street. Dore and I opened the doors and jumped out the second Dad pulled to a stop. Mom's hair was still damp, and I caught a strong whiff of her rosemary mint shampoo as she wrapped her arms around us. It smelled like home.

"Babies!" Tears pooled in her eyes. "I've missed you so much!"

"We missed you too, Mom," I whispered. "*Mahal kita.*"

"*Mahal kita,*" Mom whispered back.

Lola Marita was waiting inside for us, her tiny body almost swallowed up by the puffy armchair she sat on. I moved toward her but paused mid-step. I never saw her except on a computer screen, so it was awkward for about two seconds, until she smiled with that familiar gleam in her eyes and winked at me. "Well, don't stand there, Lizza. Come give your favorite grandma a hug. Right now!"

Dore beat me to her, which surprised all of us, and *Lola* Marita loved it. She cried, too, seeing us in person for the first time since Dore was a baby.

The Strickers fed us blueberry pancakes and Mom told us all about her mom's heart attack, while *Lola* kept cracking jokes that made Mr. Stricker blush and Mrs. Stricker laugh out loud.

"I like you Americans." *Lola* sipped her orange juice. "You eat dessert for breakfast. My heart doctor wouldn't approve but I say never mind! I want to live it up once in a while."

Mom told me to help the Strickers with the dishes while she, Dad, and *Lola* talked outside. Frowning, I did what I was told, moving in slow motion. They were leaving me out of their discussion of the cave-house situation, but why couldn't I be there? Wasn't I a part of this, too? So, I cracked open a window to eavesdrop.

Mrs. Stricker had other plans for me.

"How's life at Hole N' the Rock, Lizza?" she said in her big, booming voice. I winced and tried to lean closer to the window as I scrubbed syrup-sticky plates.

"Okay." I strained to listen to the voices outside. *Lola* Marita was talking.

My heart attack was minor, but they need to put a stent in one of my arteries...

"Mr. Stricker and I miss you all terribly," Mrs. Stricker said, while she wiped off glasses and stuck them in the cupboard.

"Uh huh," I murmured.

I haven't seen my grandchildren in so long, so that decided it. Besides, you have a nice new hospital and good doctors—

"I worry about that sweet brother of yours living so far out of town and unsupervised all day long," Mrs. Stricker added.

I leaned closer to the window. This time, Mom spoke.

Sure, the cave-house is big, but there's a little crowd control problem, Clint! Mom needs quiet! How can you expect her to—?

"Oh, let's keep the window closed, honey. The air conditioning is on." Mrs. Stricker reached past me and shut the window, her round arm brushing against my ear.

I growled under my breath. Mrs. Stricker didn't say anything, but her husband raised one eyebrow above his newspaper.

When the doorbell rang, Mrs. Stricker sent me to answer it since her husband's sciatica was "acting up" and he didn't want to move around too much.

Noah stood on the front step, his blue eyes round in his tanned face as he looked up at me.

"Hey," I said. "How'd you know I was here?"

"Mom said. I got a bird." His face was serious.

"That's nice," I said. "What kind is it?"

"A bubble gum bird," he said. "Here."

Like I always did, I held out my hands for the invisible animal. And Noah put something tiny and soft in them. A real baby bird, naked and pink, quivered in my hand. It did look a lot like a chewed-up piece of bubble gum.

"*Coconuts*," I whispered. "Where did you find this?"

"Under our tree," Noah told me. "Bye." With his face now wearing a wide grin, he jumped down from the Strickers' front steps and ran home.

I ducked back inside. Mrs. Stricker hummed from somewhere down the hall and Mr. Stricker wasn't in sight. The others were still in the back yard. In the kitchen, I found an almost empty matchbox, put some wadded-up tissues inside, and stuck the tiny bird in there.

"It's okay, little guy," I said. "I'll take care of you." I poked holes in the lid of the matchbox and closed it to keep the tiny bird as warm as I could. Then I hurried back to the front door, reaching it right as someone knocked.

I opened the door. Tona.

Oh...coconuts.

"Hi." Guilt smacked me on the back of the head.

"Hi." Tona's hands were in his pockets and his eyebrows drew together, just like Noah's had a few minutes ago, when the kid had given me the tiny bird.

"Do you want to come in?"

"I actually came here to see you, Lizza," he said. "Can we talk?"

We went outside and sat on the porch while a thousand butterflies fluttered inside me. Tona leaned forward with his elbows on his knees, keeping his eyes on the street. I held my matchbox bird in my lap.

"I've always liked you, Lizza," Tona said, without looking at me. "Your parents were great to me when I first moved here and needed a little help. Do you remember?"

I nodded, glad I didn't have to try to squeeze any words past the huge lump in my throat. Tona's house was robbed after he'd only been here for a week. His place got trashed and he lost most of his stuff. My parents, the Strickers, and a bunch of other neighbors got together and fixed his broken window and the things that got broken inside the house. They even got him some new furniture.

"That's one reason I stayed here," Tona said. "I felt at home right away. This neighborhood is a real community. It's like a family, almost. That's why I always let your Dad borrow my tools."

My mind raced. What could I tell Tona? What *should* I tell him? The truth would get me into huge trouble. Add that to the list of everything else I'd done, and I was toast.

Tona didn't say anything else for a minute or two. The morning sun was already growing hot, and sweat dripped down my sides from my armpits. I shifted around but couldn't figure out what to say. The tiny bird made soft, rustling noises inside the box.

"Look, Lizza, I'm going to level with you. I saw you take my ladder the night before your Dad's billboard got vandalized," Tona said in a soft voice. "I figured you needed it. Then, I forgot all about it until I saw a photo of it online and learned someone used it to ruin your dad's sign."

"We needed the ladder to clean the gutters." I lowered my eyes. That was true. Sort of. We always needed to clean our gutters. I needed time to figure this out, and Tona wasn't giving me any!

Tona shook his head. "I can't help thinking the police believe *I* was the vandal. They have no other leads except for a partial print that doesn't match my fingerprints. I'm not supposed to leave town until this is solved." He sighed and cracked his knuckles. "I told them I thought it was overkill to say I couldn't go anywhere, but, well, I guess it's because I have a record. Nothing big, you know," he added, glancing over at me.

"What did you do?" I asked.

Tona's shoulders slumped.

"I had a little too much fun on my twenty-first birthday," he said. "Got into my car when I shouldn't have. Nobody got hurt, but I crashed into the side of MC's and busted the wall, along with my old Pinto."

"That was you?" The incident at the nearby corner store was famous. Brooklyn and I loved to go to MC's and raid the ice cream cooler for popsicles or frozen lemonade on a hot day. At least, we used to, when I still lived in this neighborhood.

"Yeah," Tona said, rubbing his hand over his head. "I did a few days in jail and earned a fine that took a couple of years to pay. Now I'm not just one of Moab's few black guys, I'm *that black guy*—the trouble maker. I'm not surprised the cops suspect I defaced the sign, but of course I didn't do it, Liz," he said softly. "Do you have any idea who did?" He turned to me and stared with this intense expression that made my stomach curl up around my pancakes.

I wanted to tell him. I really did. But I couldn't. Not with everything else that had happened in the past couple of weeks.

"I don't know what happened to it," I said. "It disappeared from our yard the day after I took it from your garage. I was afraid to tell you because I didn't want to get in trouble for losing your ladder."

The tiny bird made the tiniest of squeaking sounds, like it was scolding me for my lie.

Behind us, the screen door opened with a loud squeal. I jumped.

"Tona," Mr. Stricker said with a big smile. "Come on in."

"Thanks, but I have to go. I just came to say 'hi' to Lizza," Tona said.

Mr. Stricker nodded and ducked back inside. Tona stood and headed down the front walk, but he turned around after only a few steps.

"I was about to propose to my girlfriend, but I can't right now with this legal trouble hanging over my head," he said. "Not until it's resolved and I know I'm not suspected of vandalizing a billboard. If I want to get married, I can't afford another big fine. Or more jail time." He stood there and gazed at me, to let the words sink in, I guess. They did, all right. They plowed through me and sank right to my toes. It hurt.

"Well," Tona said after a second or two, "say hi to my girlfriend for me when you head back to work. If she's still my girlfriend, anyway. We got in a big fight about this."

I swallowed hard. "Your girlfriend?"

"Yeah," Tona said. "You know, Zochee? She talks about you all the time."

He turned and got into his jeep while I scratched at a scab on my leg until it bled. In my mind, I watched again and again as Zochee took off her name tag and covered the nickname Tona had given her.

> *Summer filled with lies,*
> *I know you don't believe me.*
> *How can I fix this?*

Thirty seconds after Tona drove off, Heidi's white Tundra pulled over to the curb and Brooklyn bounced out.

"Hey, Lizza." She rushed over to me and gave me a quick hug. "I heard you guys were here. How's your grandma doing? Hey, what's this?" Her words tumbled out, practically tripping over each other.

I blinked back tears and cleared my throat. "She's all right, I guess. And this is a baby bird I just found."

I opened the match box to show her the tiny pink animal inside.

"Aw, it's so cute," she said. "But I thought you weren't supposed to do any more rescuing for a while."

I put the lid back on the box. "I know." I stared at the ground.

Brooklyn put a hand on my arm. "What's wrong, Lizza?" She frowned. "Are you okay?"

I glanced behind us to make sure the front door was closed. "It's Tona." I cradled the matchbox in my hands. I couldn't manage lifting my eyes to my friend's face. "He saw us take his ladder."

Brooklyn took a step back. "What?" Her voice ended in a squeak. "Oh. My. *Heck!* He knows you ruined the billboard?"

"Not exactly." I licked my dry lips and cleared my throat. "I told him we took the ladder to clean our gutters."

"You lied to him?" Brooklyn's eyebrows drew together and I pulled the matchbox closer to my chest.

"I couldn't tell him, Brooks! He's already upset because he says the police think he was the one who ruined the billboard." I stood and headed down the walkway toward the street.

"That's why you need to tell the truth, right away!" Brooklyn said, catching up. "You can't let him take the blame for this."

My eyes stung. Tona was my friend. Not like Brooklyn, of course. I was only twelve and he was a grownup. But he always treated me like I was an equal instead of some annoying kid from the neighborhood. I took a deep breath. I didn't *want* Tona to be blamed for this, but I had no choice!

Sniffing and biting my lip, I reached our Explorer and grabbed my backpack from the back seat. There was no way I could tell everyone what had happened. It would ruin everything. With shaky hands, I tucked the matchbox inside and carefully put the pack on my shoulder. I'd have to keep the box hidden, and hopefully keep the tiny bird quiet, until we got back to Hole N' the Rock. Then, I'd find a place for the little guy to go.

"Are you even listening to me?" Brooklyn asked.

"I am," I said. "Really. But I can't get in any more trouble, Brooks." I turned to face her. "My life is crazy." I blinked back tears. "Mom's back but she and *Lola* aren't staying with us. I don't know what's going to happen. I don't even know if my parents will ever live in the same place again. They're so mad at each other, Brooklyn! I can't make things worse by telling everybody what I did. You understand, don't you?"

Brooklyn looked at me. She just stood there staring with her green eyes droopy and sad. Her eyes kept moving back and forth between the backpack on my shoulder and my face, darting like a bird trying to catch something too fast for it.

"I don't get it, Lizza," Brooklyn finally said, shaking her head. "You're only doing stuff that will make things worse, not better! You're taking in another rescue animal when your mom said not to, and you're just going to let Tona get in trouble."

"He won't." I scowled. An instant later, my flash of temper flared out and left me with a tightness in my chest that made it hard to breathe. There was no way I could actually be sure Tona wouldn't get in trouble. I gulped. "Besides, what else can I do?"

"You can tell the truth!" Brooklyn said. She crossed her arms and glared at me.

I jerked my head back like I'd just gotten smacked in the face. Didn't Brooklyn understand? I didn't want to hurt Tona, but I was stuck in an impossible situation. "I can't, Brooks," I said in a trembling voice.

"Yes, you can! Let Tona off the hook, and maybe stop trying to make your dad move somewhere else. He *likes* Hole N' the Rock, and the place isn't all that bad!"

"Are you kidding?" I blurted. "My great-grandparents are buried right outside my house, which, by the way, happens to be a *cave*, Brooks."

Brooklyn gasped. "Your great-grandparents? As in the Christenson's? They're your family?"

Oh, Scooby snacks. I cursed to myself and lowered my head. Why did I tell her that?

My friend's eyes filled with tears. "I can't believe you never told me, Lizza. Why didn't you?" Her face puckered.

"I couldn't," I said. "It was way too embarrassing."

Brooklyn whirled and walked back to her mom's Tundra. "I've told you tons of embarrassing things," she said in a voice rough with tears. "Because I trusted you. And I thought you trusted me." She paused, holding the vehicle door open. "I have to go. I don't want to be here anymore."

My mouth hung open. "I thought you were my friend."

Brooklyn got into the vehicle. "I *am* your friend, but I can't go along with what you're doing. Not when you're hurting your family and your friends. Not if you're going to get me in trouble along with you." She slammed the door.

Heidi came out of the Strickers' garage, where she'd probably been stuck looking at Mr. Stricker's new electric car. She gave me a hug and asked me if I was okay. I nodded, but I couldn't talk, because my insides were turning into mush. When Brooklyn's mom got into her Tundra and started the engine, I turned my back and walked down the sidewalk. I glanced at the vehicle when it passed me. Heidi was scowling. I ducked my head.

We were two best friends
But something went really wrong.
I don't understand.

I hid in my old back yard and cried. When I stopped blubbering, the tiny bird cheeped at me every few seconds. It had to be hungry. So, even though my face was all red and puffy and my heart was shredded into a million pieces, I got up to feed the little guy.

The door of our old storage shed wasn't locked, so I took a quick peek inside. We used to keep bird seed in there, and a crumpled bag was still on a shelf. I found a handful of seeds in the bottom, so I scooped them out and went back to the Strickers' house. Everybody was outside, so I crept into the kitchen.

A drinking glass worked to crush the seeds. The mashed birdseed made a brown sludge when I mixed it with warm water, but the bird didn't mind. I dribbled a bunch of it all over him with a spoon. At least some of it got into his tiny open beak, and he finally stopped chirping after a while and closed his round eyes.

Brooklyn would have loved doing this. I blinked back tears as I cleaned up the rest of the mushy baby bird food. I hadn't even had time to ask her how Rosie was doing.

The sleeping bird stayed hidden in its matchbox home inside my backpack. I hung out with the Strickers and watched a boring old-people show about an old lady detective. *Lola* Marita helped Mrs. Stricker make sandwiches for lunch. Nobody ate much. Mom and Dad stayed in the backyard and talked some more, but at least by the afternoon, they weren't yelling. Mom even laughed, once.

We grabbed a pizza that night and sat under a tree at the park to eat. I picked at a slice of my cheese-free veggie pizza. It was my favorite, but tonight I might as well have been chewing on paper. Mom kept looking at me. She could tell I wasn't okay, but she was too busy with Dore to talk to me much. He wouldn't leave her side, and he wouldn't let go of Spiderman, either.

"It took us a year to get him to put that thing down," Mom said with a sigh.

Lola loved Moab and she kept saying it. She loved the green city park, the souvenir shops lining Main Street, and said the desert was one of the most beautiful places she'd ever seen.

"Moab is wonderful," *Lola* said in between bites of pizza. "I expect to see John Wayne walk by any second now." She grinned and patted her short dark hair streaked with gray. "Or at least a cute cowboy. I should check my lipstick. Anybody got a mirror?"

"John Wayne's dead, Marita," my Dad mumbled around his food.

"So what?" *Lola* said. "I bet he's still hot." She winked at me and I couldn't help smiling at my grandmother, a tiny old lady who talked like a teenager. My late grandfather, my *lolo,* had been obsessed with old Western movies where cowboys rode around on horses and got into gunfights. A bunch of those movies were actually filmed nearby, a long time ago. People still came here to visit those places. And my *Lola* Marita was sure she'd get to meet a real live cowboy in Moab.

"John Wayne's real name was Marion Morrison," Dad

said to no one in particular before taking another huge bite of his pizza.

Mom laughed out loud and *Lola* Marita tossed a bit of crust at Dad but missed.

"Real life isn't like those old Westerns you used to watch, Mom," my mother said, smiling at her. "Farmers and ranchers live around here, of course, but you're probably not going to see an actual—"

"Cowboy!" *Lola* shouted. We all laughed when she got up and walked over to a twenty-something guy wearing Wranglers and boots. He even had a big brown Stetson on his head.

His round cheeks flushed red when *Lola* hugged him and asked to take a picture. But soon he smiled right along with her. They took selfies together. The guy had to crouch down low so he and *Lola* were the same height.

And then, the most amazing thing happened. Mom laughed and put her arm around Dad.

"My mamma is so crazy," she said.

"Your mother is so wonderful," Dad said. "I'm thrilled she's going to be okay."

And Mom kissed Dad's cheek. It happened so fast you could have almost missed it, but it happened. Mom pulled away and went back to wrestling with my little brother. Dad smiled, a really happy smile that practically glowed like sunlight, and took another bite of his pizza. The breath I'd been holding whooshed out of me in a long sigh. My parents still loved each other. It was going to be okay.

My grandma said goodbye to her cowboy and came back to our picnic spot. She sat down and put her arms around me, and I leaned into the hug. She was magic. Somehow, *Lola* Marita had the power to make everything better. I only wished she could help me figure out what to do about the cave-house. And Tona's ladder. And Brooklyn. But at least Mom and Dad weren't still mad at each other.

"Oh, Dore," Mom said. He'd taken his shirt off again. I noticed the tag sticking out from the back collar. I'd somehow missed that one when I removed the tags from Dore's other shirts.

"Oh, we need to cut the tag off," I told Mom. "Then it won't bother him." *Lola* handed me some nail scissors from her purse and I snipped off the scratchy bit of material. I held the shirt out to Dore, and he smiled at me and let me help him slip it over his head.

Both of my parents stared at me with their mouths hanging open. My face got hot. Kids screamed and splashed at the pool nearby, and a young couple with a baby walked past us, softly speaking in Spanish. Finally, Mom cleared her throat.

"I feel kind of dumb," she said. "All these years I've wrestled with this kid to keep his clothes on." She stopped and laughed softly. "It never occurred to me that the tags might bother him."

"That's such a great idea, Liz," Dad said with a big grin. "How did you figure it out?"

"I, um." I gulped.

Oh, pond scum! The signed papers! I sat up straight. Now was not a good time to tell them about the papers. Not yet, anyway. I settled for telling part of the truth. After all, they hadn't actually asked if I'd signed anything lately.

"I got the idea from Mrs. Barlow," I said. "She came by one day to talk. She told me about how Dore kept his clothes on at school because they gave him soft clothes with no tags to wear when he got there."

"Oh, they did, did they." Mom's eyebrows met in the middle. "I don't remember being asked for permission to put my child in clothing that didn't belong to him." She got up and gathered scattered plates and napkins. "That woman drives me crazy. The whole school year she would not shut up about the testing, no matter how many times I said no."

Uh oh. Suddenly, I couldn't look anybody in the face. Once my parents found out about the papers I'd signed, I'd be grounded until I was sixty-five. Why couldn't Mom just be happy about something that helped my brother?

"You know, I think we've both been a little too hard on Mrs. Barlow." Dad finished his pizza and picked up the box. "I mean, look, Daph, Dore's keeping his shirt on! I never made the connection either, you know, about the scratchy tags. His teacher only wants to help him. Don't you think we could—"

"No," Mom said in a voice loud enough to send a couple of birds fluttering away from the branches above our heads. She jumped to her feet and dumped garbage into a can nearby. "All that woman ever wanted last year was to label my kid so she could stick him in a room by himself and keep him away from all the other kids. That is *not* going to happen, Clint!"

"But I'm sure it won't be that way, Daphne," Dad said. Mom's phone rang. Dad turned his back and ran a hand over his face while Mom looked at her screen.

"Speak of the devil," she muttered. "It's *her*."

My hands turned to ice.

Mom answered her phone, walking a few steps away from us. Her face was a thundercloud.

"He signed *what?*" Mom said. Dad stared with his mouth open.

Lola took me and Dore to the car. We waited in the heat while sweat trickled down my back. Mom and Dad talked for a long time. Dad kept shrugging and shaking his head.

His red face twisted with confusion. Mom's was twisted with fury. Finally, they walked our way.

As Dad opened the door, I caught a few words.

"—keep telling you, I never signed anything," he said.

"Well, she says you did," Mom hissed.

They climbed into the Explorer. Dad turned the ignition, the engine roared to life, and we drove off. Mom kept her face turned away from my father.

I stared down at my worn-out sneakers. Mom blamed Dad for signing the papers. And of course, he wasn't the one who signed them. *I* was.

"Let's go to the cave-house," *Lola* said in a voice that was way too happy. "I'm so excited to see it." But even *Lola* couldn't get us to smile.

Dad shrugged and kept driving. Mom said nothing. The only sound was the hiss of the air conditioner as we drove.

I can't let Mom keep believing that Dad signed those papers. But, how could I tell my parents what really happened? I was already in so much trouble!

You did the same thing to Tona, you know, my brain reminded me. *You're letting him take the blame for something you did.*

Biting my nails, I tried to stop thinking about everything that had happened, but I couldn't. And one thing kept sticking out in my mind more than anything else: Zochee's name tag, and how she'd covered up the nickname Tona had given her.

I'd hurt my dad, I'd hurt Tona, and without meaning to I'd even hurt Zochee. I'd dragged Brooklyn along with me to paint over the numbers on Dad's sign, not thinking of how much trouble I could get my best friend into. And it was all my fault that our garage burned down. We didn't live in a cave because of my dad. We lived in a cave because of me.

Stupid conscience. It totally would not leave me alone. I was letting everybody else take the blame for me. And I couldn't keep doing that.

The drive back to Hole N' the Rock took, like, thirty years. I held my backpack with my new little friend hidden inside. I kept sneaking peeks at the matchbox, wishing the tiny bird could tell me what to say. When we were almost there, I took a deep breath, ready to spill my guts. Dad turned the Explorer into the parking lot and slammed on the brakes. He cursed out loud. So did Mom, in Tagalog.

More protestors had shown up at Hole N' the Rock. Like, a lot more. I couldn't even count how many people were crammed inside the parking lot. The roar of their voices was like the sound of a heavy rainstorm. Dad could hardly move the Explorer through the crowd to park.

"You have *got* to be kidding me," Dad muttered under his breath.

The red-headed woman I'd spoken to caught my eye and waved, smiling big like we were best friends.

I sank down in my seat. And for a second, I actually held my breath and closed my eyes like I used to when I was three and believed it would make me invisible.

Sometimes I still really wished that would work.

M om, *Lola,* Dore, and I squeezed and squirmed through the crowd to get inside the cave. I ducked into my bedroom and put the baby bird on a small shelf carved into the wall. I fed him more mushy birdseed and put a warming pad under the matchbox. He snuggled down inside the tissues and closed his teeny eyes. Total cuteness.

"Albert," I whispered to him. "That will be your name." Since he was going to live in Great-Grandpa Albert's prehistoric house, the name fit. I watched baby bird Albert for a few minutes while he slept, putting off what I had to do.

"Mom?" I called, finally leaving my bedroom. My mom, *Lola,* and Dore all stood inside the dusty living room by Zombie Donkey and stared out the windows. Dad waited for the police outside. "Mom? Can I talk to you?"

"Not now." Mom didn't take her eyes off the scene outside the window.

No more than ten feet away from us, a guy held up a sign reading, "All meat comes from the dead." Below him, a girl laid on a big white tray, covered in clear plastic, and splattered with what looked like blood. I hoped she had air holes to breathe through. She saw me looking and moved her hand in a tiny wave. Tiny because she could barely move her arm within the tight plastic wrap.

"I'm going out to take pictures," *Lola* said. "My friends won't believe this!"

"But Mama—" my mom said.

"No buts," *Lola* said. "I'm out of here." Giggling, she went outside with her phone.

Mom, Dore, and I stayed where we were. *Lola* took a lot of selfies with the protestors. And she kept hugging a bald man who had leopard spots tattooed all over his body—either that or he'd gotten creative with a Sharpie.

"Wow, she really likes that guy," I said in a quiet voice.

"Well," Mom said with a sigh, "she does love cats." Dore giggled.

We took turns reading some of the signs out loud.

KEEP IT NATURAL: LEAVE NO FOOTPRINTS
(OR GIANT LETTERS)

BAG CRUELTY: DITCH LEATHER

WOULD YOU STUFF GRANDMA AND PUT HER IN
YOUR LIVING ROOM?

"*Good point*," I whispered to myself.

Just then, Zochee pushed through the swinging doors.

"Hey," she said. "Sorry to bother you, but a woman is asking for Mr. or Mrs. Crapo. She's waiting in the shop."

"Who is she?" Mom asked.

"She said she was from something called 'DCFS.'"

Mom gasped. My guts turned hard inside of me, like one of dad's freeze-dried poodles.

DCFS stood for The Department of Child and Family Services. They were the ones who took your kids away if they believed the kids were in danger.

"Shizzle sticks!" I said out loud.

"Stay here with Dore." Mom followed Zochee into the shop.

Gulping, I held Dore's hand tight while my thoughts banged around in my head like a pair of sneakers whirling in a clothes dryer. The social worker was here because of me. Someone must have read the survey where I'd posted photos of my new home and called social services to report my parents. Every single photo I'd taken flashed through my mind: the bucket filled with rusty nails, the gross toilet, the electric wires all over the floor, and the scary close-ups of Zombie Donkey.

Crud muffins. I'd totally made my home look really, really bad when I'd posted the survey about the cave-house. Wincing, I kicked at a dust bunny on the floor. I'd never even read the results.

I didn't have a phone, but Mom did, and she'd left her purse on the floor next to the dead donkey. Glancing around to make sure Dore and I were alone, I fished it out of her purse and logged on to my social media site.

*Survey: Does this look like a safe place for kids to
live in?
Results:
Yes: 17%
No: 83%
Comment: Where is this?
Comment: Completely unsafe living conditions!
Poor kids.
Comment: Someone could really get hurt, and those
cords are going to start a fire.
Comment: I'm calling the police.*

There were a lot more comments like that. I closed the app and dropped the phone like it burned my fingers. Brooklyn had been right when she said I might get my parents in trouble. Brooklyn was right about a lot of things.

Dore put his arms around me and squeezed. Closing my eyes, I hugged him back, ignoring the tears running down my face. I'd been trying so hard to manage my life over the past few weeks, but right then, something finally hit me. I wasn't managing *my* life—I'd been trying to manage everyone else's lives. And all that got me was a whole lot of trouble. Not just for myself, but for the people I loved the most.

Swiping my arm across my face, I picked up the cell phone again. Dialing the number I knew by heart, I apologized to Brooklyn in my usual oddball way, meaning I wrote a haiku and texted it to her.

> *Ladders and surveys,*
> *Everything you said was right.*
> *Please forgive me Brooks.*

Shoving the phone into my back pocket, I pulled Dore into another hug. I hadn't noticed until then, but my hands shook. Were we about to be taken away from our parents?

Outside, *Lola* was still taking selfies with protestors. In the souvenir shop, Mom's voice got super loud. Dore hugged me even tighter. I bit my lip so hard it hurt.

And at that moment, a massive tour bus pulled into the parking lot. It inched forward while the flood of protestors parted into two big clumps, almost like a giant slug being cut in half.

"Fudge nuggets!" I shrieked. It was Clint Brown's tour bus.

I couldn't breathe. A picture of the superstar singer's supersized face covered the side of the long bus.

Lola slapped her hands over her mouth. Then, she jumped up and down. I wasn't sure someone who'd just had a heart attack should do that.

"Come on, Dore," I said. "Let's go outside." The front door, usually locked tight, gave a squeak and a groan as it opened, but it finally let us out. We hurried over to *Lola*, who shrieked like a teenager at a concert.

"I know him!" She grabbed my arm. "He's a singer. Oh, he's so cute! Let's go meet him!"

She took my arm and dragged me, along with Dore, into the crowd.

A burly driver guy with dark glasses waved people away from the bus, but they didn't budge. Dad weaseled through the crowd and talked to the big guy. Instead of telling him to get lost, which is what I totally expected to happen, the guy smiled. And then he actually let my dad pass by.

Right then, a tall skinny man wearing black jeans and a gray hoodie popped through the door of the bus.

"Clint!" he shouted.

"Clint!" my dad yelled back. Then, no lie, they hugged each other.

Lola screamed in delight and clapped her hands. The crowd jabbered all around us while *Lola* took a photo of my dad hugging Clint Brown. I stood there with my jaw hanging down to the ground. If an entire hive of killer bees flew into my mouth at that moment, I would not have noticed.

Dad and Clint slapped each other on the back three or four times.

"So good to see ya, man," Clint Brown said when the slapping finally died down and they moved apart.

"You too, bud," Dad said. "I love the billboard! Have you checked it out, yet?"

"Not yet," Clint said. "Just drove up from Colorado, but I saw the photo you sent. Looks great!"

As all the people swarmed around Dad and Clint, elbowing and shoving, Dore and I got separated from *Lola* and squeezed out of the group. Within ten seconds, we stood together out by the chain link fence at the front edge of the parking lot.

We looked at each other.

"I did not expect that," I told my brother. He smiled at me.

"Bus," he said.

Mom's phone buzzed, telling me I had a text. It was Brooklyn, answering my apology. When I read her words, my heart fluttered like a hummingbird on Mountain Dew.

Thanks for the haiku. I told my parents everything. Sorry.

I'd figured as much. Still, my stomach churned. Brooklyn's parents were probably going to tell my parents the whole story, if they hadn't already. I took a deep breath and reminded myself this was what needed to happen. I had to stop *managing* everything.

And then another text appeared.

We're on our way.

Glancing at the crowd of protestors, the bus, and the souvenir shop—where Mom was probably arguing with the social worker lady—I bit my lip. This was not going to be fun. I needed to get away from the crowd so I could think.

"Let's go see Chewie, Dore," I told the kid. Still smiling, he followed me as we squeezed our way through and around the crowd, finally making it to the trees where Doug parked his trailer.

A tan woman with long auburn hair stood in front of the wire enclosure where the raccoon lived. Her hand was on the wide-open gate. A dark, furry blur shot toward the trees and disappeared.

"No," I shouted, running up to the woman. "She can't live in the wild. She might die out there."

The woman brushed her hair off her shoulders. She smirked at me in that annoying way some adults do when they talk to kids. "She'll be fine, honey," she said, putting a hand on my shoulder. "She doesn't belong in a cage."

And then she walked back toward the crowd, picking up a sign that read: *End All Animal Oppression.*

Dore burst into tears. "Chewie!" he sobbed. And before I could stop him, he pulled his hand from mine and sprinted into the trees.

"NO!" I shouted, but he didn't look back. In seconds, he was out of sight.

ore didn't answer my shouts. With tears streaming down my face, I ran through the trees, looking wildly all around me. There was no sign of a little boy with curly hair wearing a superhero t-shirt.

Sniffling, I pushed through the crowd and went to find Mom.

When I got to the door of the shop, someone called my name. I turned just as Brooklyn ran over and threw her arms around me.

"I'm so sorry," she said. "It was killing me not to be honest with my parents."

"It's okay," I mumbled against her fluffy hair. Pulling back, I swiped my nose with my arm. "But listen, Brooks, Dore ran away! Please, you've got to help me find him."

Brooklyn put a hand over her mouth and her eyes grew round. "Where could he be?"

Someone screamed and Brooklyn and I both jumped. Other voices shouted, and then a man yelled, "There's a kid up there!"

My world stopped. "No," I sobbed. Grabbing Brooklyn's hand, I ran far enough into the lot so I could look up to the top of my home.

My brother's tiny figure sat above the cave-house on the level shelf where I'd climbed a few days ago. He was huddled there with his arms folded tightly around his knees. I let out another sob.

"This is all my fault," I said. "I never told Doug to put the ladder away." That stupid, impossibly tall ladder still stood in place next to Roosevelt's head, all because I'd forgotten about it. I was too busy being mad at my dad. Brooklyn put her arm around me and my eyes went blurry with tears.

Mom burst out of the souvenir shop, talking fast in a panicked voice, mixing English and Tagalog.

I swiped my streaming eyes. "I have to go get him."

"Come on," Brooklyn told me. She grabbed my arm and together we ran to the base of the ladder.

"Be careful," she told me as I put a foot onto the first rung. As I climbed, cool raindrops splashed onto my face. They pinged on the metal rungs and water fell faster and faster until the rain made a soft, roaring sound. People in the crowd shouted, "Stay where you are! Don't move! Someone's coming!"

When I got to the top of the ladder, the crowd cheered. I eased my way onto the rock that was getting slippery from the rain and got down on hands and knees, creeping toward my brother. When I reached him, Dore turned a tearful face to me.

"Chewie," he said.

"I know, buddy," I said in a soft voice. "We'll find her. I promise."

Scooting next to my brother, I put my arm around him. Smiling and sniffing, he leaned forward and pointed. In the rain-filled air, the people in the parking lot below appeared as just a wet blob of soft colors, their movement like bobbing waves. And the shining tour bus was like a ship floating in the middle of a colorful ocean.

"Bus," Dore said, just like he had earlier in the parking lot.

"Bus," I said with a sigh.

Dore snuggled into my side and we sat, just for a minute, in the soft, pattering rain while red and blue lights from arriving police cars flashed on and off below us. It was peaceful and kind of pretty. While we sat, I didn't think, or talk, or worry. Relief and love washed over me and spread through me. Dore was okay. The world was okay. Soon, though, my clammy clothes stuck to me and I shivered. Everything was not okay. Not yet. There were still some things I needed to do. Besides, people were yelling at us to come down.

Dore and I crawled back to the ladder. Just in time, since a fire truck eased its way into the parking lot. I didn't want anyone to get the idea that I had to be rescued, or anything. I had my pride. What was left of it, anyway.

The clean smell of rain filled the air while I helped my little brother climb down the ladder. The crowd hushed to a low murmur as we inched our way back to the ground. My parents, Brooklyn, and *Lola* Marita waited at the bottom.

When Dore saw them, he scrambled like a lemur down the last few rungs and flew into their arms. Mom held him to her and sobbed. Dad's mouth was wobbly, the way it got whenever he tried not to show his emotions but was about to lose the battle. I stayed right where I was for a second, as still as Zombie Donkey.

Everybody looked up at me, including my parents, who clung to my little brother; my best friend, who hugged herself and cried; and my tiny *lola,* who stayed quiet for once. Then, there were the police officers and fire fighters; Clint Brown, the country singer, who stood there with his muscle-y driver; and all the protestors. Even the guy with leopard spots on his face gaped at me, and so did the girl from the giant meat tray, finally out from under her plastic wrap. Zochee stood there, too, with her wet hair all over her face. And, *gulp,* so did Tona. Tona? When had he gotten here?

Fizzing gizzards!

"I'm sorry," I yelled. "Okay?"

"Lizza, just come down," Dad said.

"Not yet," I said. "I have to tell you something."

"It can wait," Mom said. "Please, honey, come down."

"No!" I yelled. "Tona, listen. I *did* borrow your ladder. I'm the one who ruined Dad's sign, okay? Not you."

A slow smile spread across his face. He mouthed the words, *thank you.*

"Now the police know, too. You can marry Zochee," I told him.

His smile froze. Then, he started to laugh. He turned to Zochee and knelt down on one knee on the wet pavement.

The only sound was the soft whir of traffic going by. It was like every single person in the crowd held his or her breath. Zochee kept glancing up at me and then back down at Tona. But then her face crumpled a little and she nodded and smiled. People in the crowd cheered, and Tona and Zochee wrapped themselves in each other's arms.

Moving a few rungs lower so I wouldn't have to keep yelling, I caught Dad's eye.

"I didn't mean to ruin your sign," I said. "I just wanted to change the number. But I almost fell so I reached for something to hold on to. That's how I tore the sign. It wasn't on purpose. I promise."

Dad shook his head. "Oh, Lizza."

"It was also my fault the garage burned down," I added, before I could lose my nerve.

Dad kept his head down for a few seconds. He rubbed the back of his neck. "It was that raccoon, wasn't it?" he asked, finally looking up at me with a half-smile.

"Yeah," I said. "I freed her from the trap. I'm so sorry, Dad. I didn't mean for anything bad to happen. Honest." I sniffled and broke down. "I never thought it would be a problem. But then we had to move, and you and Mom—"

Dad held his hands out for me, so I climbed off the ladder and into his arms. I couldn't remember the last time he'd hugged me like that. It made me cry harder.

"*Mahal kita*, Lizza," Dad whispered into my hair. "Thank you."

"*Mahal kita*, Dad," I said, snuffling all over his shirt. "But there's one more thing."

"No more for now," *Lola* announced. "You kids need to get inside and get warm. I say we go hang out with that singer."

Everybody laughed, even Clint Brown.

"I like that idea," he said. "You heard the lady, Clint. Why don't you and your family come on in?"

I pulled away from Dad's shirt long enough to say, "And Brooklyn, too."

Dad chuckled. "Brooklyn, too."

Clint Brown's tour bus was like a slightly smaller version of Brooklyn's house stuck on wheels. He had a huge TV and his furniture smelled new.

"Why didn't you ever tell me your dad was friends with Clint Brown?" Brooklyn whispered to me. My friend and I sat together on a huge sofa. Mom sat across from us in a cushy chair. Dore snuggled on her lap, smiling. Dad paced the narrow room and cracked his knuckles.

"I didn't know," I whispered back. I kept shaking my head. I mean, my dad was friends with a huge celebrity, and he'd never told us! Not a word. Of course, he listened to the guy's music every single day, but he never once dropped us a clue that he actually *knew* Clint Brown.

My best friend couldn't stop staring at the singer, who was making nachos for us. *Lola* Marita helped him. She sat on a bar stool and flirted while she chopped green onions. She'd already asked him if he was single.

Mom stroked Dore's hair but her eyes were on me. She wasn't wearing her "mad face," but she didn't look away from me, either, even for a second. I tried to ignore it but I could have sworn lasers were burning the top of my head while I kept my eyes on my feet.

Dad stopped pacing. "Your tour bus is amazing, Clint," he said. "Can't wait to see what your house is like." The singer grinned over at him.

"I'm where I am today thanks to you, man. I'll never forget that," he said.

Brooklyn and I looked at each other with wide eyes. The country singer saw it. He walked over to us and put a huge platter of nachos on a little table.

"I mean it," he said. "Your dad and I were roommates in college. Life wasn't too good for me back then. After my girlfriend broke up with me, I kinda got lost for a while. I turned into someone I didn't recognize. Lost my scholarship *and* got kicked out of my own band, the one I started myself." He paused to take a sip of Coke. "I thought life wasn't worth anything anymore. But your dad saw where I was headed, and he set me straight."

Clint clapped a hand on Dad's shoulder. My dad's face turned bright pink. Mom's eyes got shiny with tears.

"Clinton Crapo is the best man I've ever known," the singer said. "I owe him my life. And if that means I get to help him out once in a while by letting him use my ugly old face on a billboard, well, it's the least I can do." He winked at me.

Dad turned to me. "A new billboard that will not be ruined, accidentally or otherwise, right, Liz?"

If I could have magically disappeared into the zebra pattern on the couch, I would have.

"Of course not," I mumbled.

"But that sign is the least of my worries." Dad ran fingers through his hair, making it stand on end. "I have a bit of a problem with that crowd out there. They're disrupting my business. But what's worse is, Daph says we might be in trouble with the state, since social services is now concerned about the safety of our kids."

"Seeing both of our kids up on the tall rock probably didn't help, either," Mom said in a quiet voice.

I winced. "I know." I cleared my throat. "Uh, so, Dad? Remember when I said I had more to tell you?"

Dad turned to me and folded his arms. "I'm all ears."

"So am I," said Mom.

Staring at the floor, I told everyone about my house photos and how I made our oddball home look really bad and unsafe.

"That's why the social worker was here today," I said.

Dad slapped his forehead. Mom rubbed her temples, gently put Dore off her lap and headed to the kitchen area so she could take some aspirin. A tear ran down her face. *Lola* hugged her.

Clint Brown suddenly remembered he needed to talk to his driver and left the bus.

"Lizza," Mom said, sitting down by me and putting her arm around me. "You did something that could really make it hard for our family. If the state thinks a place is dangerous for kids, they might take them away and put them in a foster home. Do you understand?"

"Yes," I whispered. "But I didn't think that would happen. I just wanted to move back into a real house."

Dad paced back and forth, cracking his knuckles. "Was that the reason for your silly bathtub snorkeling show? And why you gave Roosevelt a nose ring?"

I nodded while my face burned. "I think the protestors are here because of me, too. Brooklyn and I made a video that went viral, and I guess people also saw the stuff I posted about the environment and animal rights."

Lola whistled. "Wow." She took a sip of her lemonade. "But I was about to tell you not to worry, Clint. I talked to them. They have a permit to be here but it's only good for three days. And the police already told them they had to move down the road. They're blocking traffic here."

"Humph," Dad grunted. He didn't stop cracking his knuckles. "Is there anything else, Lizza?"

My eyes filled with tears. Brooklyn squeezed my arm.

"Yes, Dad," I said. "We're a family. We all need to be together. You, Mom, Dore, and me."

"Did you forget someone?" *Lola* Marita called, planting her hands on her hips. "I'm here, too, Lizza!"

"And *Lola*," I said with a tiny laugh. "Can't we find a way to stay together? Please? I'll live in the cave if Mom and *Lola* are there with us. I'll even live above Dad's taxidermy shop."

Whoa. That fact was totally news to me until the second I said it. I sat there, blinking, taking it in. Maybe my dad stuffed dead animals, and maybe he'd bought us a totally tacky cave, but he was still my dad. Mom was my mom and Dore was the best little brother I could ever have. Lola Marita was an awesome grandma. And without them, my life wouldn't be the same. I sniffed and *Lola* brought me a tissue and kissed the top of my head.

"Oh, Lizza," Mom said softly. "This is all a little complicated. I'm afraid there isn't an easy solution."

"But it's not hard," I said. "You and Dad love each other, right?"

"Yes," she said, after a quick, teary glance at my dad. "But we also have to be able to trust each other." Dad closed his eyes and turned away.

The papers. I had one more thing to do.

"Just don't kill me, okay?" I whispered to my parents. They glanced at each other and then at me.

"What is it this time?" Dad finally asked with a sigh.

So, I told them.

For a second, we all just sat there, waiting. Brooklyn's eyes bugged so far out of her head I was afraid they'd fall out and roll across the floor. But then Mom's face lit up and she laughed. And she jumped to her feet, grabbed my dad's face and kissed him on the lips.

She pulled away, still holding his red face with her hands. "I'm so sorry I doubted you."

Dad kissed her again, and then they just stood there for a minute, staring at each other all dopey, while *Lola* giggled and crunched tortilla chips. Dore came to sit in my lap and I hugged him, tight.

Finally, Mom turned her head and gave me her famous "Mom Look." I sank down in my seat a little.

"We'll talk later," she said.

"Uh oh, you're in for it" *Lola* winked at me. "But don't worry. I have your back. We're family, remember?"

Dore giggled.

"Family," he said.

Then suddenly, we all laughed. And maybe cried, a little. At least, I did. But this time, my tears melted away the heaviness inside.

Brooklyn went home after she got a selfie with Clint Brown. And then his tour bus eased out of the lot and headed to Moab. Mom and *Lola* went back to the Strickers' house, but they let Dore stay at Hole N' the Rock—Dad and Doug took down the humongous ladder, first, of course. And Mom promised to talk seriously about the living situation. And she hugged me really, really tight for a long time.

Just before sunset, the police made the protestors leave for the campground down the road. The meat tray girl smiled and waved at me. So did the red-headed woman, and lots of the others. By then, all the protesters had found out I was the one who made the viral video that brought attention to my other social media posts. Flushing, I waved back.

Dad and Dore went to bed early. I tried to, but everything was suddenly so quiet, nothing distracted me from worrying about Chewie. I gave up on sleep, found a flashlight and went for a walk.

The parking lot was nearly empty. It was just me, a few cars, and my thoughts. And, the statues, who for some reason suddenly seemed like old friends. I patted Mater's hood as I crossed the lot to Doug's trailer. I peeked around the back. Chewie's gate was still hanging open and she was nowhere in sight.

So, I walked into the trees, whistling for her. The sky had cleared and the sun was setting, sending pink and orange streaks across the blue. The first stars were winking and the sweet rain-scented air filled my nose. I wandered along, following the curve of the giant sandstone of my house. Leaves rustled softly, birds chirped, but no raccoon made an appearance. With a long sigh, I sat down on a fallen log.

"Can I join you?" Dad asked. His voice made me jump.

"Yeah."

He sat next to me and turned on the flashlight he'd brought. "Dore's asleep so I thought I'd help you. I heard how Doug lost his pet."

I didn't say anything. Dad didn't know who Chewie *was*, did he?

"Looks like our old raccoon was happy living out here at Hole N' the Rock," Dad said.

Tea and crumpets. He *did* know. I cringed. My dad was a lot smarter than I gave him credit for.

"Any luck finding that critter?" he asked me.

"No," I said with a sigh.

"Sorry." Dad shone the beam of the flashlight along the wall in front of us, moving it back and forth like he was searching for something.

"Hey, Dad?" I said.

"What?"

"How come you never told us about Clint Brown? About you two being friends and all? It's kind of a big deal, you know."

Dad chuckled and moved the beam of the flashlight in slow circles. "I guess it does seem odd, Lizza. It's mainly because of your mom. You know how important it is to Daphne that Dore isn't 'labeled,' don't you?"

"I did kind of get that idea," I said with a tiny laugh.

Dad chuckled and nudged me in the ribs. "Daph wants people to get to know *him*. She doesn't want others to see him as a kid with the name of a disability written in red ink across his forehead."

Ugh. Somehow, we were back to those papers I'd signed. "His teacher said the tests were just to help him," I blurted. "She really cares about him. That's why I signed the papers. Honest."

"I believe that, Lizza," Dad said, patting my arm. "Let me finish. I wasn't talking about the papers. I'm trying to explain how it can be hard to see the real person behind the label you get in your head." He grinned at me. "By the way, your mom and I agreed to not make a big deal about those papers. We'll keep my name on them. Looks like Dore will get tested, soon."

"Oh," I smiled. "So, I'm not in trouble?"

"I didn't say *that*," Dad said. He chuckled when he saw my face. "What I'm trying to tell you is people are people, not labels. And the label called "fame" can be a tough one to deal with. Mom and I decided it wouldn't be good for you or your brother to be known as the kids whose dad was buddies with a big star, that's all. We just wanted your friends to like you for who you are, not who you might know. Guess that's going to change, though. I'm the one who gave Clint the go-ahead to drop by. Things have been tough. I needed a friend in my corner right now."

"Oh." I cringed. I was a big part of the reason things got so tough for my dad. But then, I smiled. "I'm so glad to know Brooklyn likes me for me." I got warm fuzzies all over. The night would have been perfect if Chewie had shown up right then. But stuff like that only happened in movies on the Disney Channel.

After a minute, Dad spoke again.

"I'm grateful to you, Lizza," he said softly. "What you told us all meant the world to me. And to your mom."

I leaned on his shoulder. I tried to think of what to say, but after a minute, I gave up. Sometimes, words weren't needed.

"Hey," Dad said. "Look at this!"

I raised my head and squinted at the spot where he aimed his flashlight. The surface of the wall was pitted and scarred, like someone had blasted it.

"We found Grandpa Albert's old Unity monument." Dad whistled. "There's the edge of the ear right over there. It's the only part of the carving left."

I sort of remembered something about the story. Dad had talked about it a few times. "Is this the sculpture the BLM blew up?" I asked.

"Yeah." Dad studied what remained of my great-grandfather's work. "Grandpa Albert wanted to carve the faces of Roosevelt and the man who was his rival for president. After Roosevelt won, the two became friends and even worked together. Grandpa wanted to celebrate their cooperation, so he carved a small sculpture here. It was just a practice run. He was going to make a much bigger one."

"Oh, yeah." Bits of the details came back to me. "It was an eagle, right?"

"An eagle with its wings spread over the faces of the two men, and under that, two hands clasped together like they were shaking," Dad said. "Grandpa said the BLM decided the sculpture wasn't on his property, so they blew it up."

"That's not fair," I said. "They were acting like bullies."

"You know something, that sure sounds a lot like someone vandalizing a billboard just because she doesn't like it." Dad elbowed me in the ribs again.

"Okay, okay, I get it," I said, laughing. I elbowed him back.

"Alrighty then," Dad said, getting to his feet. "It's too dark to search for that critter. We should call it a night."

"Back to the cave, huh?"

"Uh huh." Dad took my hand and led me along, shining the light in front of our feet. I was about to tell him I wasn't a baby and didn't need the help, but I kept quiet. It was kind of nice.

"So, about our living situation," Dad said while we edged around a thorny bush and moved closer to the entrance of our prehistoric-style home. "Clint gave me some ideas."

My ears perked up. "What ideas?"

"How'd you like it if we put a mobile home out here, instead of making an apartment above the shop?"

I stopped short. "You'd do that for me?"

"Yup," Dad answered. "I'd do anything for my girl."

"Wow," I whispered. I cleared my throat. "Thanks." Why didn't I figure out a lot sooner what a good guy my dad was?

Dad heaved a big sigh. "Besides that, a mobile home will probably look like a much safer place to live compared to the cave-house. At least it will according to that social worker, who's for darn sure going to come back."

I ducked my head. "Yeah."

Doug came jogging over right as we were opening the door of the souvenir shop.

"I found her," he said with a big grin. "Well, she found me. Chewie came back and curled up in her bed."

"Yes!" I shouted. "Call the Disney channel!" I didn't even care how silly my words sounded.

Dad grinned. "Glad she's back. By the way, Doug, I've

got a big job for you. Let's get started with that idea of yours."

Doug's face split into a wide grin. "Sure thing," He turned back to his trailer. "But I can't take credit for anything. It was Lizza's idea," he called over his shoulder. "Night!"

"What is he talking about?" I asked.

"We'll talk about it in the morning," Dad said.

"But—"

"Get some sleep, Lizza," was all Dad would tell me. "I'll explain it tomorrow."

"You're going to love it," Doug called.

"Promise?" I called after him.

"Promise."

I closed the gate in the new fence Doug built and made sure to latch it. Then, I stood back and read the nearby sign again.

Hole N' the Rock Animal Sanctuary

It still made me smile. We'd opened our sanctuary only a week ago, one month after the "Child Climbs to the Top of Giant Rock Formation" headline appeared in our local papers. The story even made it to the TV news broadcast that night.

Doug told me he got the idea from me when we'd sat on top of my house. I'd pointed out the open area with lots of space for animals. I *knew* I liked that guy!

So far, our sanctuary was the home for a miniature pony who'd been abandoned, an ostrich recovering from an accident with a four-wheeler, and a camel named Fred whose owners had died. And of course, our old friends Chewie and Priscilla. We figured we'd get more animals, sooner or later. Only ones who needed a home and couldn't live in the wild on their own, of course.

The sanctuary brought in more tourists, making Dad happy. But some of the former protestors came back with new permits. That did not make Dad happy. But then, he figured out that any time someone with a sign showed up, so did people from the local news. And then, more tourists came. So, he didn't mind any more. And the crowd never got as big as it had that first night. The guy with the leopard spots even thanked us for opening a sanctuary.

"Hi, Lizza," *Lola* said, squelching over to me wearing the old swim fins. "I was a big hit with this group!" We high-fived each other. *Lola* and Mom drove to Hole N' the Rock each day, and *Lola* led some of the house tours while Mom did the books. *Lola* did the bathtub snorkeling act at least once every day. Her photo was in the local paper last week.

"Want some help?" I asked, as *Lola* sat on the bench next to me and tried to remove the pesky fins.

"Sure, Lizard," *Lola* said, grinning at me while I pulled the frog feet off her tiny human ones. "*Salamat.*"

"You're welcome," I said. "And why are you calling me 'lizard'?"

"Don't you like it?" she said, laughing.

"You've never called me that before," I told her, yanking at the swim fins.

But *Lola* didn't answer. Instead, she said, "This Friday I want to go with Dore to the riding center. Why don't you come along, too?"

The therapeutic riding center was something Mrs. Barlow suggested, and Mom agreed to it. Once a week, he went to a place in Durango where he rode horses while therapists worked with him. We still didn't use labels. Dore was just Dore, my funny, goofy, sweet, and amazing little brother.

"I'd love to," I said.

My tiny grandmother took the swim fins from me. "I'm so excited he's talking more! I don't understand how those horses help him do that, but I'm glad it's working."

"Me, too."

Lola hurried away to lead another tour, and I leaned against the sanctuary's fence and smiled at the weird house my great-grandfather blasted into the side of a rock formation in the desert. Okay, I still lived inside a cave, but I wouldn't for much longer. Our new house on wheels was coming soon. It was a double-wide mobile home. Dore and I would each have our own bedroom. And we'd all be together. Dore, me, Mom, and Dad. And *Lola*, who decided to stay for a while.

I'd chosen the perfect spot for our new house. It was a quarter mile away from Hole N' the Rock, in a place surrounded by a few tall cottonwoods. It wasn't far from Great-Grandpa Albert's unity monument, but definitely inside our property lines—Dad checked. We'd have a perfect view of the land around us and the turquoise sky above.

Brooklyn's mom pulled into the parking lot, and my friend jumped out and ran over to tackle me with a hug. "Hey, Lizard," she said, poking me in the ribs. "How's it going!"

"Why is everyone calling me 'Lizard' today?" I asked. "*Lola* just called me that."

Brooklyn's eyes twinkled. She brushed her bangs away from her sunburned face and grinned. "You'll see."

"See what?" I said. Just then, Dad came out of the shop with Mom and *Lola*, who held Dore's hand.

"Oh, good, you're here," he said to Brooklyn. "Think she's ready?"

Why were they all grinning at me? I folded my arms, but Brooklyn just giggled and took me by the shoulders. Then, she spun me around.

"What are you doing?" I asked.

"Look up," she told me.

Then, I saw it: a giant green lizard. It was a sculpture about twelve feet long, stuck to the stone high above the souvenir shop. It looked exactly like a scaly lizard scrambling over the red wall of my cave-house. How did I miss *that*?

"It's 'Lizza Lizard,'" *Lola* said, clapping her hands. Everyone laughed.

Dad grinned at my surprised expression. "I found it on eBay and I just had to get it. It reminds me of you."

I hugged him. "Thanks, Dad."

After putting some frozen pizzas in the oven, Brooklyn and I went back outside to pour birdseed into the feeder I'd hung near the door of the souvenir shop. It was for baby bird Albert. He'd already graduated from his little box nest in my cave bedroom. Albert was actually a "black throated gray warbler," and he had beautiful, soft feathers.

Also, he was a *she*. Doug told me.

My feathery friend found herself a home close by. If I waited for her under the pine trees and whistled, she'd fly to me and land on my finger, cocking her head and chirping. Her black button eyes always seemed to be laughing.

Of course, she needed a new name. I called her Gladys.

> *Caves, dolls, and lizards*
> *Friends, family, birds and sky.*
> *I have a new home.*

Acknowledgments

I owe gratitude to a number of people who helped me during the creation of this book. First of all, many thanks to my 2016 Pitch Wars mentors, Abby Cooper and Gail Nall, for helping me create stronger characters and a better story overall. Their support and enthusiasm for Lizza and her unique world helped keep me going. I'm grateful to Cara Tinio, who read my story and made suggestions regarding the Tagalog language and wonderful culture of the Philippines. Any inaccuracies in the book are mine. I'm also grateful to many writing friends who were willing to read draft after draft, particularly Spring Paul, who has gone through my manuscript more times than I can count. I also owe my thanks to online writing friends who have commented and given suggestions so often over the past few years, including Amber Buckley, Spencer Hoadley and Kristina Ursenbach. Finally, thanks to Holli Anderson for being a thoughtful editor, and to the staff at Immortal Works for bringing this book to life!

About the Author

Rebecca Bischoff is the author of two previous novels, including a contemporary YA story titled *The French Impressionist,* and *The Grave Digger,* a historical middle grade mystery. Rebecca loves to read everything from mysteries to paranormal to historical novels. She has a tendency to research quirky and little-known facts from the past, and loves anything that might make her laugh. Rebecca lives in Southern Idaho with her family, where she enjoys *not* visiting the outdoors. She'd rather stay inside, eat chocolate and write. Visit her website at: www.rebeccabischoffbooks.com.

This has been an
Immortal Production